QUANTUM

Published by Perigee Press

Paperback ISBN: 978-1-7392083-2-5
eBook ISBN: 978-1-7392083-3-2

Cover design and typeset by SpiffingCovers

QUANTUM

ROY MAGARA

Book One of the Quantum Trilogy

To those who dare to dream.

CHAPTER ONE
Into the Veil – Part I

We fell.

With the light rising higher with every second, I flipped back – the air billowing at every angle around me – dodged a poking rock and landed. Ripples of soft dust cast a wave from me There were whispers that soon turned into an echo. The noises that swept across the underground floors seemed to bring an icy chill alongside the scurry of rats that scrambled across the slippery surface. If you turned around, you could see another dead end and, looking up, the Watery Veil that separated this world from the next.

It was almost clear now, but trying to focus felt as much of a chore as it was to stand up straight. All around me, the sides of the walls seemed to be held with jagged rocks and skeletal bones. As I walked forward, the smell changed. What was once neutral was now a gust of sour, acrid air. It seemed to engulf all of my senses. I thought of turning back, but now was not the time for quitting.

The sound of dripping water appeared unexpectedly as I walked forward – deeper. The light faded through the dust. The wetness somehow managed to bite through my brown, leather shoes. As I entered knee-high water, thoughts of what horrid creatures might dwell within materialised… I heard a scream – familiar to me.

My heart raced…

I turned around. I noticed that she was still behind me. In the dim light, even now, I could see that locks of her long, brown hair had taken a route of their own across her face. She looked at me with emerald-green eyes that spoke louder than the alarm that had so suddenly left her mouth, which she was now clasping with one hand.

I motioned an expression as if to say, "Are you okay?". She clearly seemed terrified. I'd told her she didn't have to come, but she'd insisted. I could sense her heart racing, almost as fast as mine, as she showed me the bony hand that had clutched her arm from the dark surface below her. Was it another message? I thought of light, and immediately everything was clear.

"Stay close."

I looked around as I slowly motioned through the underground maze.

Her recent skeletal captor, whom she had flung from her in haste, had drowned back to into the water. She cast her unruly hair back and managed to pull herself together. Whatever had clung on to her before had torn a bit of her light-blue T-shirt that was worn under her dark chest armour. It wasn't anything too heavy or grand. The others had given it to her hurriedly, due to her insisting on coming with me down here. Her dark, leather-like trousers were half submerged in the cave's water whilst her right hand was clasped readily to her left hip where she held her sword. It was her favourite one; one which she had often said had a purpose. It was an Albion-looking sword. The red, laced grip met the brass pommel and guard on either side. In the centre of the blade, the fuller had some sort of illegible inscription on it. I say illegible because it was in some other language which, although the alphabetical characters were what we would use in English, I had never seen or heard its make-up of dialect before.

It read, "*leqstfla disuoxus simum*".

Even the Elders were unable to decipher it. She had always stated her ignorance to it as well, but that's the kind of girl that she was; more interested in what she could do with a weapon than the weapon itself. Alas, all I could see was the pommel of the sword, as the rest of it sat in its scabbard, waiting for its time to shine.

The greeting of black, iron core surrounded us. The glimmer of moisture trickling down the side of the cave's wall was a constant feature, no matter where I looked. Behind us both was the small burst of light that fought the encompassing darkness to sustain a constant glow from where we had fallen. As I looked forward, the walls formed a tunnel that, a few hundred metres ahead, seemed to break off into other subsections of tunnels. This maze could be our grave if we ever lost our way.

My own sword was also locked in its scabbard. I was always too aware of the need to have it ready to pull out rather than have the navy blue pommel stare at me. My black trousers had stuck to my bark-brown skin now. Not that they necessarily hadn't before, but the water that had already dampened its way through the lower part of my legs was now teeming its way up, racing to my hips. A drip of water from above fell on my chest armour. The dark, rough, brown material could handle any weapon, and a drop of water was not going to be the first to penetrate it. As the drop of water worked its way down, I noticed that my long-sleeved, white cotton shirt had also begun to cling to my skin. The black, leather strap that came across my chest found its way around to my back; my arrows hadn't moved from the black, lined with gold, quiver that I had secured them in when we left. The gold fletching contrasted well with the mahogany wood sinew bridged the gap between the arrow point and nock.

I looked up, and I slowly motioned through the underground cave, signalling for her to follow suit behind me.

"*Turn back!*" Scratched marks, in consecutive groups of four, verified a poor attempt at escape, or maybe a warning? Others gave more graphic advice…

"*Walk forth and you shall die*". "*Your flesh shall be torn from limb to limb*".

It all seemed fresh. How did these people know what they were in for? Visions of helpless individuals, shouting and screaming for aid, for their lives, were unconsciously encrypted in these walls. Was the skeletal hand that clutched her earlier been yet another warning? I scanned the walls, looking for a desperate set of scratch marks, and found one. Faint marks, just above my head. I closed my eyes, let in a breath, focused and lay my fingers upon it.

*** *** *** *** ***

"No! Get away!"

As the man frantically tried to run through the water, the bubbles from below the surface seemed to draw closer to him. The man's efforts appeared hopeless, as he raced with this thing… this creature. As he stumbled on the cave floor, submerged in knee-high water, half swimming, half leaping, the flurry of his arms made the splashing of water dance tauntingly in the air around him, as the moss beneath tricked the soles of his feet into slipping at every opportunity. His wavy hair had clumped its way about his head, as his scrawny cheekbones came into focus as he turned round. You couldn't just sense the fear in his pale, grey eyes, you could see it ooze from his forehead. As he lifted up his hands in the air, grasping at dark nothings, his thinning arms were lightly capped by the shreds of his claw-torn tunic.

Suddenly, the light seemed to fade... as did his hope. He was now left in darkness. You could just about make out the eerie puffs of breath form from the pit of his lungs. But now came a different source of breath.

He could hear the faint sound of vibration, simmering under the water, getting louder and louder with each passing second. He looked up. Thousands of miles above him sat a star that twinkled in the heavens. He could almost taste the air that whistled through the small opening about thirty metres above him. With a face that at last showed a glimmer of relief, he looked about him rapidly for the cave to aid his escape up its walls.

He began to climb. But he kept slipping. His body frantically fell into the water. He was getting anxious quickly and frustration began to surround him, clouding his judgment. His clutching turned into scratching as fast as he could. I couldn't understand... Were these not concrete-hard walls? Indents began to hatch under his dirtied fingernails that were set in his prune-skinned fingers. Sooner rather than later, a snap was heard.

And then another one.

And again.

As he clenched his jaw, dark red splashes landed on the man's face. His breath deepened into what inherently turned into a scream.

But he couldn't stop trying… to get up. To get out. To get away from danger. Ignoring the nearing bubbles didn't help either, because the simmering vibrations that turned into unearthly growls began to rise like unbalanced bass music to the ear. He could hear the pop of each bubble as they surged crazily to the surface of the water. It was the kind of sound you would try and mimic by placing your lips together and blowing them out.

Pop… Pop…

He could hear them get louder as the seconds, which could possibly be his last, passed just as the wind tickled the small hairs that stood up on his ears.

The man gave up his hope of trying to climb the jagged walls, as the scream he initially gave turned into whimpers; he had finally tuned in to the sound of popping that topped the waters closing in on him. He turned and attempted to run again through the slowing water.

He felt it around his ankle. And suddenly, he lost his footing and slipped in the dark water. He attempted to scream once more for help, for something, but the water that fell into his throat broke any sound that successfully escaped from his lungs. He choked. The water that had once sought refuge in his lungs was now forced through his nose and mouth all over again. As he tried to recover, his head regained sight above the water. He continued to run, or, at least he tried to. He kicked the slippery substance from his ankle and marched forward. As he motioned ahead, the depth of the water around the dark brown shorts that covered his hips, lowered to his hairy kneecaps. You could almost make out the streaks of blood that seeped through the scratches on his calves and shins. It was hard to pinpoint exactly whether it was the jagged rocks that had caused all the cuts, or whatever it was that was under the water, or perhaps it was a mixture of both. In any event, this man knew what had caused them. The depth of the water lessened, and he came on to the cave floor that didn't harbour… the thing… the… creature that he once thought of as his tomb. He fell to his knees and just about managed to place his arms forward to stop his face from hitting the ground.

*** *** *** *** ***

There was a flash.

I seemed to have echoed the man's movements and found myself where I'd left him, lying on the hard, rough ground. I was not injured, however. I returned from my daze, as the place came into focus. I found myself at the beginning of my journey in this stone-hard abyss. As I lay on the ground, I felt the hairs on my dark-skinned left wrist flutter and part ways, turning into an itch. The legs of a giant, black ant marched its master under my sleeve and up my arm. I reached into the sleeve with my other hand and flicked the ant from me.

Her black boot came crushing down on the ant, as she stopped next to me. I saw the look on her face again; the look that asked many questions. What did I see? Who was it? Was I okay?

"What… what happened?" she stuttered. Her arms were crossed in a way that looked both like discomfort as well as consolation since no one else was there to hold her. "They told you not to do that until you could control it properly. You could have… you could have really hurt yourself." She cusped her hand below each elbow as if to hug and console herself.

"There… there was… a man. He… Those marks in the wall." I gestured with my head in the direction of the marks where I had laid my fingers. "…How did I…?"

"I don't know. You just… flung yourself…" She blinked profusely and shuffled her feet from side to side. "Are you..?"

"No," I said scanning myself, paying more attention to my nails and legs to check for any injury. Then I noticed a difference – my clothes. For some reason they were dry now; as if they had never been submerged in the water. My belt still had all of its components. My sword was still in place in its scabbard, and at the back of my belt lay the waterproof, black pouch of sift powder. I also had the packet of chocolate balls I'd picked up before I'd jumped into the momentarily transparent hole. To the left side of my hip was a space for what I had to acquire. My eyes widened, as I quickly felt my back. My bow and quiver of arrows were quietly in place. None had snapped or broken in the middle of my transition between that man's memory and the present. I let out a silent sigh of relief. Strands of her hair were scattered again abroad her face, the intermittent clouds of cold breath formed in front of her and disintegrated into the darkness above her head. A tear fell.

"Don't worry. I'm fine." I began shuffling; picking myself up from the floor. "Let's do what we came here to do." I brushed off the little stones that had clung to my clothes.

"I'll help you." She looked away from me, as she wiped the tear from her face and sniffed, moving forward to fuss over my clothes and armour about my body. I grabbed her hands and looked into her evergreen eyes. I could feel the blood pump in her fingers that were wrapped by her brown leather gloves.

"Don't worry. I'm okay." I let a smile skip across my jawline in an effort to still the quiver that had taken over her face. "You ready?" I raised my eyebrows and glinted towards the path we were yet to take.

She nodded and looked to the ground, grabbed the grip of her sword and breathed in deeply and quickly, composing herself. "Let's do this."

Pop.

Once again I sank into the water. Although I was now the same distance that I had come before, the depth of the water seemed higher. It was the kind of rise that reminded me of when I used to get into a bath and the water would come up due to the increased mass that fell into it. So what was in the water now? We both didn't weigh enough to make the water rise this high. The water was up to my chest now. I could feel the centre of my shirt begin to cling to my torso, as the water crawled in between it and my armour.

I could feel her hand clasp mine. I clutched it and squeezed it gently; in some way hoping to pass on some confidence through my fingertips.

As we travelled in the multitracked vicinity, it came to a point where I couldn't really see any more. If I placed my arm in front of me, I could just about make out the glimmer of water that slithered down my nails on to my fingers. The white sleeves of my clothing surrounded my arms, attempting to keep in as much heat as possible, as we continued our journey.

Pop... Pop...

We had gone some distance now. The level of the water currently balanced about my chest, as we waded through it. All I could hear was the dripping of water from the dark cave's ceiling falling into the underground sea of darkness, causing ripples that clashed together, and ahead, sounds of dripping that seemed to foam.

Almost like... bubbles.

CHAPTER TWO
Into the Veil - Part II

"Bubbles," I whispered.

I stopped in my tracks. My heart was now beating so hard I couldn't concentrate at all. The thumping that pulsated around my body eventually caught in my throat. Flashbacks of the man I'd seen in my vision began blitzing through my mind like a Formula One racetrack.

"Malachi... what do you mean bubbles?" I could tell that her masked face of comfort had washed away. One of the little lasers of sunlight that fought through the jagged coils of rock, in this spire of a cave, cut across her face to show all of her muscles forcing themselves not to crumble.

"What do you mean bubbles?"

"Can't you hear it? Shush... Listen."

Neither of us sought to make any movement. But at that moment in time, such drastic, statue pretences were unnecessary. The sound of the popping grew louder and closer, and if she couldn't hear it, she certainly needed her ears checked again. Galen clearly didn't do a good job since...

"Oh... What is that?" Her eyes began to widen, as I could see the variety of possibilities display in her mind.

"We need to go," I said, moving backwards. "Now!" As we quickly made our way through the water, I could feel the moss under the soles of our feet constantly try to slide us into the water and entangle us in this mire until the enemy revealed itself. Whatever it was that had caught our scent, I could feel the past vision and present experiences merging, as if that man and I were sharing the same experiences, intertwined into the same fate of utter loss.

She let out a cry of frustration, as she slipped and regained her balance; just like the man that I'd seen in my vision. The height of the water had lowered a bit now up to my hips. But I was 6 foot 3. She was a good few inches smaller than me and so the water that was currently up to her chest was causing more drag than assistance to her. My mind was too occupied to even think of the time that we'd…

"It's too far!" she cried, as she turned to face me for a split second. A lot could be gathered from her facial expression mixed with both inquisition and fear. I opened my mouth to tell her to keep going, that everything would be okay, but I slipped into the water. The breath that I had initially taken to exhale comfort and encouragement transformed into a mouth filled with a taste of murky mud and underwater salt.

I just about raised my head again, regaining my feet, when I heard her say, "I see a gap above here." She looked up and pointed to the side of the wall. "We can climb."

Pop. Pop. Pop.

I brushed the water off of my face with my hand and saw her begin to try and scale the wall of the cave to safety. She was about eight or so metres ahead of me at this point and, before I could gather my thoughts, she began to feel for cracks and folds in the wall.

She fell, her arms still reaching for the wall, as she splashed into the water.

"Damn it!" she choked. "I can't get a freakin' grip on the walls!"

Occurring in almost slow motion, I could see the semi-transparent image of the man merge himself with her shape. I could see the scurry of his fingers across the granite-black walls that offered no hand to the oppressed. I then saw him turn to me. Everything was a bit misplaced now. It was like an oddly tuned orchestra playing the finale of a dark musical piece. Composure had to be resurrected somehow, but it was as if the band was playing autonomously without the direction of a conductor. I saw her turn to me. As she turned back to the walls, she began to scratch. I knew what would happen if she continued to do so.

"Stop." I blinked back into focus. I marched through the water towards her. She was too lost in the darkness of her own thoughts to hear me. "Stop!"

Grabbing her hands, I looked into her eyes. They were veiled in a wall of tears that swelled up in front of her eyes. This veil then opened up a waterfall down her pale, rosy cheeks.

"We need to continue and go now." I put my hands on her shoulders and looked into her eyes, forcing her to concentrate on me. I had never seen her this scared before. I could only conclude that the effect of what happened at the…

"It's going to be like the others," she said. "Like the…" The fear grasped her lips once more. She used her hand to pull down slightly the neck of her T-shirt where the clean cut was still visible. It had now turned into a scab, but the purple, red and blue surroundings only brought back memories that the scars were not all that old. The scar was one I knew well. I knew how it got there. It mismatched the natural cream complexion of her skin which, in the trace of light, was paler than usual.

"What happened to whoever you saw earlier in the vision?" She brushed her hair aside and sought to establish composure in her stature. You could barely notice the freckles that grazed up her arm, as if someone had dipped their fingertips in coffee and flicked them at a painting. It is what made her kind of cute. But now was not the time to reminisce of such things.

"I don't know. I didn't get that far."

"The vision… the… the… Malachi! What did you…?"

"Not now!" The last thing I wanted to do was scare her even more. "Let's go." I turned her around and pushed her forward; ushering her to go ahead of me.

We rushed through the water. It was so hard to move at normal pace. I couldn't dare swim. I wouldn't know what would grab my ankles without the support of what little gravity I had, and the noise the additional splashing would make would certainly not work in our favour. Chessboard-splashed light cast their rays upon the waters, aiding me to finally make out the sludge around my shoes.

And then it happened.

I felt the slippery substance, slicker than the water underneath, coil around my ankle. A flashback of the man I saw in my vision returned. I could see the angst in his face; the terror and anguish perspire through his temples. Before I gave myself the opportunity to do the same, I reached for my side and gripped my sword. I thrust my foot back and forth, trying to fight it off in the process. The smooth, swift chime of my sword against the scabbard resounded and bounced off the cave walls, as I thrust it under the water around my ankle. The black grip was firmly placed in my hand. The blade sliced through the water, seeking to taste the next casualty of its titanium edge.

Pop. Pop. Pop.

I looked down. I saw part of something, something that looked slimy on its own account, regardless of the water's own liquid features. It was like oil in a puddle that was swirling like an unruly nucleus. There seemed to be a wavery essence that hovered around what let go of my ankle at last. As it slipped back into the darkness, the essence swirled into nothingness and dissolved into the water. I know I just tried to tell you what it looked like but, you know what... I couldn't really describe it; it was like the gases that encircle a flame from a cigarette lighter, but without the scent.

I looked a little bit further down the pool, and I noticed something that was not there before. Steam perhaps? Smoke? Out of the little light that cut through the jagged, black curtain, I beheld what seemed to be heated water flowing towards me. But the part of the water which I was standing in was not exactly boiling. In fact, I was rather cold. The ghastly fog flowed in our direction and, as my focus turned back to the water a few metres in front of me, I noticed that it was turning to ice. We began to move back.

The stampede of snowy ice pulses towards us like a cavalry of white horses; their icy breath fuming out of their noses like a steam train. What was even odder about this whole process was that the apparent steam seemed to be erupting from the icy surface. The cannons from underneath seemed to be blasting their way through the icy plain that was slithering across the water. What was causing this?

The breathing heightened, and then it hit me. Thinking of the vision I'd had earlier, we were close to the end of this underwater siege. All we had to do was get on to dry land, right?

Pop. Pop. Pop.

Movement… Little pebbles, hailing from above, began to fall around us. They appeared to crumble under the sudden changes in temperature and bursts of lava that erupted from the watery volcano.

"They are here. Somewhere…" she shouted, waving her hand about her face as the little, black stones that brushed her features fell into the water. "I don't know where though. What if it is…?"

"No. The Laden wouldn't be here. But we need to go. We can't just stop and stare and die here. We need to get on to dry land… There!" I said, pointing in the direction of the tunnel where I wanted her to run. "Well, drier than where my knees currently are anyway!"

Trying to sound comical was the only solution I had to lifting her rumbling trepidation, and distracting whatever else was going on in her head.

The chase began. The notion of being a mouse chased by a cat was emasculating, but not knowing what I was running from was frightening!

I looked around.

In that moment, I saw them; simmering eyes under the water. In fact, there were two pairs of them. The first were fiery red, glaring like iron cast in a furnace. The second pair of eyes could only be described as Antarctic blue, a seal of frost freezing whatever was before it. Whatever it was, there were two of them!

"Go! Go!"

Before I could shout any other form of instruction or encouragement, I heard boulders crashing and thundering echoes of dust and tremors up ahead.

Our route was blocked. Where were we supposed to go now!

Pop. Pop. Pop.

I turned around again. Whatever these eyes were part of, they were joined by what looked like neck. Scaly sheets of copper slates and mercury blue veins merged into one larger body which shimmered and intermittently glowed from scorching orange to electric blue.

"It's blocked! We are stuck!" She reached the caved in tunnel path ahead of me first and began to try and move the rocks that stood guard to our only escape. I, on the other hand, had to stay focused.

With only the slight glow of the barely visible body under the water, to me, it was obvious which way we had to run. I broke out of my daze and let my legs take action.

"That's fine…"

It wasn't. In fact, it really wasn't fine. That was the only route I knew that would get us to dry land! The falling stones and rocks from the ceiling were no aid to our quest to get to dry land. The volume of the water rose instead. And we were so close.

"Right! Go right!" I flagged my arm frantically. By this point, I had caught up with her. She was paying no attention to what I was saying, focusing too much on moving the glued wall of denial before her.

I grabbed her forearm; her racing pulse emanated through my fingers. She let out a gasp, as I pulled her away and dragged her behind me.

The water was dangerously close to her neck at this point, and I could tell that she was struggling.

"The amulet…" she said.

My left hand reached for my neck.

"I haven't used it since Jared…"

I had a moment of silence as I remember the…

"Malachi!"

She was practically treading across the water and the falling debris from above was offering no assistance. I had to focus.

I could feel the wavery glass amulet around my moist neck, held by the silver chain that clung around it. I looked at the endless yards of water in front of me. I could tell she was noting my eyes turn grey. Nimbus clouds appeared to have engulfed my eyes, as a wind picked up from nowhere. Well, not just nowhere; by the power of the amulet, of course.

"Are you ready?"

She nodded.

I lifted my other hand ahead of me, and an invisible line cut through the water in front of me.

"Separate."

The water split in two like the Red Sea did for Moses as God led them through to the Promised Land. The ground ahead of us breathed its first sigh of air, showing us the paths, the rocks, the moss, the holes and the glistening, black granite rock that we had been treading upon all this time.

We ran. For the first time, we actually ran. I had to remain mentally focused in order to keep the water (which had flung itself upon the cave walls) parted! The falling stones and rocks were now ticking on the black ceiling, as the wind from the amulet defied the rules of gravity.

Not the complete mass of water was separated, however. Only what was in front of me was exiled from its previous abode. The water behind us was beginning to crash down upon itself. The barrage of water was now resounding in our ears, pounding together as it returned to a whole.

The eruption of steam and cracking of ice was nearing behind us.

"Ah!" I just about heard her scream in the midst of the discord.

I turned around. She had fallen. The splattered mud and little stones had clung on to her face now, as her wet, brown hair sprawled across her forehead, cheeks and eyes. Perhaps she had tripped over a rock. Or maybe something had tripped her?

Her breathing was heavy, as she began to try and get up. She was only a couple of metres behind me. I could see a tear in her trousers simply because her white skin was slit across her knee, and pulsing red droplets formed across the gap in her skin.

I lost my focus, let go of the amulet and ran towards her. At this point, I hadn't begun to notice the water starting to fall around us; like bulls from both sides running towards us; us being the big, red cloth waved by the taunters. I couldn't just leave her there, though.

As I crouched down next to her and cuddled my arm about her, I began helping her to her feet.

"My knee." She placed a hand carefully around her left knee. The splashes of black, blue and red danced around her wound as she winced. She wasn't crying. Oh no, she was a tough girl. But it looked like the fall really had done something to her knee which caused her to limp, as she struggled to get up. I glanced before me, to the ground and then ahead of me again in disbelief. The water was falling fast in front of us like a tidal wave darting towards its targets. Like a movie scene, my world seemed to slow down.

With her arm around my neck, she was still struggling to gain any speed due to her injured knee. The water was closing in and was gushing forward; it was only a few metres before we were smashed by the current on either side, swept off our feet into impending destruction and failure.

I reached for my amulet and shot my other hand forward.

My eyes flashed grey, and in a quick moment, the wall of water halted centimetres in front of our faces. A spiral of water was facing my palm. The roaring water, the foam, the black spots within the water, all of these were fighting against the force holding it at bay; seeking to finally quench its thirst with our bodies.

I flung my forearm back, bending my elbow, and shot my arm forward again, this time slicing my hand down through the air, and shouted, "Separate!"

Once again, the water was cast against either side of us.

The… thing under the water wasn't far behind either now. It couldn't be too far. And just as I turned my head around to check the same, I saw something peer out, just before the water behind us crashed down. I saw the copper scales that led to the bleached white talon that sparkled in the water which brushed against it and then evaporated. I had to concentrate.

Now was not the time to worry about what was behind us. I mean, don't get me wrong, it was certainly a very good time to worry about creatures with talons and copper scales, but she was more important at the moment. I had to get us to safety as quickly as possible. If only she had stayed in Safety Net! She would not have, as bad as it sounds, been a liability. I looked forward, and we continued to gallop along the murky ground ahead in this underground metro tunnel.

Pop. Pop. Pop.

"You'll be fine. Just keep going."

I was sure the Watery Veil was somewhere up ahead in the maze if we could only redirect ourselves. But we couldn't let whatever it was track us through. It wasn't safe. Not after what happened when...

"The sift powder," she said through gritted teeth.

"Not now. We haven't got enough to use twice. It's not that far ahead," I said. "We can still make it. You need to fight through the pain in your knee."

My world returned to normal speed, and we were back on the race to safety; the panting of our breath was echoing through the cave. The violently crashing water a few feet behind us was being crackled and popped by the unidentified creature that was further beyond.

"Kai, my leg..."

But there was another item I had to get from this place before we went. That's why we were here.

Pop. Pop. Pop.

Well yes, that's what the gap by my left hip was for. They'd told me it was the only way I was going to have the upper hand and defeat...

"Malachi, I can't..."

She collapsed on the floor. The cut on her leg was oozing out red rivers that clung to her leather-like trousers and smeared down on to the ground. I let go of the amulet and focused my attention on her, as I tried to get her to her feet. The cloudy vapour that surrounded my eyes disappeared, as my mahogany irises and dark pupils set their focus on her.

The flames burst through the heated water as, in the next moment, shards of ice showered the ground. Sweat and droplets of water were raining down my face, as I looked around me. The humidity in the air swam through my nostrils, as I realised we didn't have enough time. The water was coming in too fast. The crashing, clapping, clattering waves echoed around us.

I reached for the back of my belt and fumbled about for the black pouch. The string was girdled protectively around the mouth of the little bag. I had to get in. It was either that or certain death. I felt the little globe in my fingers; no bigger than a golf ball. Inside the marble and Jupiter colour-swirled globe was the sift powder. I crushed the ball in my hand and cast it about us.

And in a spark of light, and in my case a flash of disappointment, we orbed.

CHAPTER THREE
Family Tree

As the sun shone its radiant rays down to the earth on that bright summer's day, the scattered children, stroppy teenagers and bustling adults began to swarm on to the beach like a herd of possessed rhinos. Strips of golden sand danced upon the visitors' feet as they hopped from toe to toe, to be carried by a gentle, gallant breeze to a foreign part of the caramel, gritty sheet which led to the playful, clear blue sea that ushered back and forth.

The heavens had declared that today was a day where the nimbus clouds would not hang their dreary dictatorship over the earth. The seagulls played competitively in the air; their squawking joining the cheery chorus of souls below. The fresh ocean air drove carelessly through the aerial highways; swerving through the legs and fur of the many dogs that barked uncontrollably in excitement across the sand. Their owners fussed over them and gave them their just desserts for the many strops and moans placed on replay throughout the cold, windy winter. The red frisbee spiralled through the air, cutting across the crowds to metres far, where the leaping, blonde-haired teenager would dive in the air, catching the frisbee in his hand and gambolling across the ground, losing his footing and falling over in laughter; noting that his pink-laced, bikini-wearing girlfriend had lost faith in her aspiring knight in shining armour. Her dainty laughter attracted the attention of a horde of nearby children building their first of many sand dens; claiming a fortress to deter all the imaginary evil armies who would seek to take over their new kingdom.

What this entourage of new, budding soldiers weren't able to see was one excitedly thrown American football that barrelled its way from the heavens to the centre of the so recently built empire. The fireworks of glistening sand surrounded the bemused children, as one little girl let out a whimper. She, in her little, multiflowered, purple and yellow beachwear and matching enveloping hat, rose out of the defeated sand dune and she marched towards the open arms of her resting mother.

Further down the stretch of beach, a swarm of yellow and black, buzzing bees had broken rank and sought the drip-dropping ice cream that melted off the mountainous cream, caramel cones; the sweet scent seduced their wings to flutter farther and farther. One bee lost track and fluttered across the ear of a father who was already struggling to carry his family's belongings across the sandy field, as they darted off to find the best plot of the beach. The buzz across his ear was met with a shaggy shaking of his head, causing his slick, black sunglasses to hang loosely across his sunburnt, Rudolf-red nose; his hands were clearly out of further service too. The bleached white parasol, tucked under his arm, rested on the blue, red and white beach sheets that were perched across the array of straw picnic baskets and white towels. His cream linen shorts and white and khaki shirt were competing for the viewer's attention whilst his mahogany sandals wrapped around the soles of his feet; sharing what space there was left with the warm, gritty sand.

His tightly curled black hair became a homing spot for the crazy bee. His trimmed sideburns were the bridge for his moustache to encircle his dry mouth and lips. His huffing and puffing was clearly visible in the flaring of his nostrils, as his dark black eyes crossed over in an attempt to hypnotise his glasses back to their original home.

His cries to his darling wife were completely ignored – caught in the wind – as she chased after her two cubs with an endless array of water bottles, slow downs and hats. Her thirteen-year-old son looked back at the lioness from the thirty or so yards that he was from her. Their mother clung on to her sandy brown beach hat that bobbed up and down on her long, black, straight hair. Her African-black skin glowed gloriously in the sunlight, as she battled with the offbeat strands of hair that sought refuge in her nose and red-lipped mouth. The wind created pseudo Mexican waves about her silky, black blouse and white satin dress.

"Jared! Be careful please!"

The younger cub displaced his mother's worries; chasing after the older, faster lad in front of him. He wore only white swimming trunks as his clothing, which made the splattered splodges of sand ever the more visible; like brown paint sprinkled on a white sheet of parchment. He, with his mocha-brown skin and piercing brown eyes, zoned in on his target. He leaped over the ageing couple seeking silent solitude from the younger, noisy crowd; the sprinkles of sand on their faces and necks alerted them to their foiled plan, as the sun's light was briefly eclipsed by the alien body above their heads.

The parasol hit the powdered sand.

"Alici… Oh that woman…"

He grunted about himself as he squatted down, attempting to pick up the wandering item.

"Alicia! A bit of help would be nice!"

The hot, golden sand pierced though the older cub's foot. He charged through the crowd wearing a tight, white cotton T-shirt and bold blue shorts. He too, with his oak-brown skin, relaxed and crew cut black hair and bark-brown eyes, long jumped over a sandcastle under construction by the team of little builders and landed on the target to which he claimed 'their spot'.

"Found it!"

As he roared across to the rest of the nearing pride, his younger brother pounced through the air and tackled him to the ground. They rolled across the ground in laughter, as the younger cub tried to secure his older brother in a headlock.

"C'mon, Jared! Is that all you got?"

"I'm winning this time!"

The sprinkles of crystallised earth rose in the air around them, as their legs darted off in all directions, seeking to fortify their place in the ground to sustain their victory. They rose, facing each other, one metre apart, in a Texas gun showdown. The younger cub dove at the other but missed, as the older swiftly strode to the side. He grabbed the younger's flailing arm and hooked it around, jerking Jared back to the ground and locking his head in the sand with his knee.

"Do you give up?"

A muffled 'no' permeated from the sand, as Jared struggled to find a free limb to come to his aid.

"Malachi Valeriano! Let go of your brother at once!"

The warning cry from his mother signalled to the older lad that now was a good time to let his competitor go.

"You are acting like a pair of lions! Come on now. I have been calling you, and you just don't listen."

She began fussing over her sons, mainly Jared, swiping off the shimmers of sand about his body, as he massaged his neck and arm into peaceful mobility.

"We were just playing, Mum."

"Go help your father, Malachi."

So I went. Yeah, Malachi. That's me. Malachi Valeriano. I was just about to enjoy the first summer holiday away with my family in a long while. The past few years had been tough. Dad had been busy working his backside off only to lose his job a few years ago. Having gone to a good university and with two decades of experience as a managing director of a bank, you would have thought getting another job wouldn't have been so hard.

Well… it probably might have been a bit easier if it hadn't been his bank that actually fell into liquidation. His board had promised him that their new investments would protect their assets in the impending doom that had taken over the global headlines. The investments, by one of his board members, Judas, happened to be embezzlement and the fine that the English courts placed upon his entity gave him no other choice but to relinquish his pride and joy that he had worked so hard to establish. Mum had always sought to warn Dad about Judas, whom she often nicknamed Iscariot, always quoting bits of Scripture from the Bible and telling him that he seemed as deceitful as Judas Iscariot, and often said that one day he would betray him. That year was not the best year to say 'I told you so' though.

Two days later in the same year, his matriarchal mother in Spain had passed away. Some coward sought to snatch her elbow-held, favourite handbag as she walked home alone down the one street from the World War II Remembrance Day service at the local church building in the November night. In the semi-tone, lamp-post-lit street, the whole experience climaxed into a sudden cardiac arrest that left her lying alone on the cold, gravelled ground in Alcobendas, north of Madrid. Her attacker took what little she had and cast the bag upon the cornering street. The telephone call to my dad broke him.

It was such an awful time for my dad. Having to watch him go from a proud king of his jungle at home to a forest sloth in a few days was no easy feat. Jared was only seven years old then. It was not exactly like he understood a lot. I was eleven. Yeah, I know. It is not exactly the age of all wisdom, but I certainly saw a difference in him.

I remember the day so well. I had just been driven to my friend Mark's house for his eleventh birthday party on Tiverton Drive. The teenage years were dawning, and the additional number of glowing candles on the frosted chocolate cake that his beaming father had brought in were a simple sign that we were growing up and were soon old enough to join the Power Rangers we had so excitedly watched in the years gone by. I was the black one and Mark was the blue ranger. We would often team up at break times at school and fight the forces of darkness otherwise known as my other gang of formidable friends who were clearly just as cool.

Mrs Hendricks, the curly, ginger-haired mother, tiptoed to the ringing black phone as we all played hide-and-seek in the downstairs, dimly lit conservatory. I can remember

Tracy Summers trying to fit in the cubed, corduroy, cream-coloured poof. Chubby Duncan Allen was attempting to play stick insect by the equally thinly stemmed, brown-legged lamp that stood inconspicuously in the corner of the glass-walled room. Brian Jeffries, with his fluorescent orange hooded top and grey tracksuit bottoms, had opted for the behind-the-curtain option. Needless to say, by the wiggly toes that played the wooden floor like a piano through his rainbow-coloured socks, he was the first one to be found. I can remember Mrs Hendricks, in her sunflower-yellow, floor-flowing dress and curtain, cut and sewn, white and blue-flowered apron.

Her smile turned into a controlled look of sudden sorrow as she looked at me, put the phone down on the Victorian oak cabinet, which was covered with an array of family photos and achievements, and told me that, "Mummy is coming for you again, as she needs you to go home."

I remember the days I would come home from school and find him on the same dark leather couch I'd left him on in the dawn of the morning. His Mediterranean skin had lost its olive complexion, as he wasn't eating properly (nor was he going outside). He would play with the bulky remote control in his rugged hand, switching from channel to channel, staring through the grey box rather than actually watching anything. It was not like he wanted us to see him like that. At least, that is what Mum told us. It was simply because the world never gave him a lucky break.

I would often hear her tell Simeon, my dad, that where she came from in Uganda, there would be people begging on streets and villages with no running water. We were in fact the blessed ones! She did not say it to him in a way that ever sought to patronise him but, I guess, to bring his world into perspective that, actually, her job as a midwife in the local hospital was bringing in enough income to keep things running for a while.

Alas, Mum eventually forced him to shave his beard which was growing in shaggy proportions. The brighter side of the coin eventually showed, and Dad ironically got a call from one of his competitors, telling him that they wanted him aboard their capitalising Bank of Commerce. You could almost say he felt like a man again. He enjoyed the buzz of getting up in the morning; wearing his slick, sharp black suit, ostentatious range of ties and leather shoes. He would skip into the chandelier-lit dining room and kiss Jared and I on our heads before smooching Mum and grabbing a piece of crusty toast before waving his jet-black-skinned briefcase in a majestic goodbye and buzzing out of the door. Having to impress the new bankers came with the price of working late, though.

The long hours would leave Mum desolate without the warm company of her husband, and I was always able to note the way she would stay up at night waiting for him to get back. She would wait in her silky, silver gown by the sombre living room, glowing lamp reading her 'Word of the Day' and pondering on the same for the minutes to follow. Dad would, eventually, silently get back and delicately place the clinking latch on the heavy wooden door. I would, by this point, be in my single, quilted bed. But I could hear the 'Sorry I'm late' and 'I promise I will get back earlier tomorrows' repeatedly sung from my father's lips met with the 'I'm trying to understand and be considerate' and 'let's just go to beds'.

One night, I remember creeping out of my room and standing by the dimly lit hallway of our three-bedroomed house. I saw how she would lovingly hold him. How she would whisper a silent prayer in his ear; praying to the Lord Jesus and to the Heavenly Father for peace and comfort around my dad. Slowly but surely, after a year or so, things picked up.

"You alright there, Dad?"

I lifted my hand above my eyebrows, as I slowed down to the brink of my father's footsteps. I could clearly see that it wasn't working out for him, so I am not quite sure why I asked such a rhetorical question.

"Take this please, Kai."

Dad passed me the parasol, which had so clearly been bothering him, along with the bulky picnic basket with all of the refreshments that Mum and Dad had packed while Jared and I were arguing about something or other at home; I wanted to keep Mum and Dad out of the picture of this particular something and pretend like everything was just fine in front of them for the sake of peace. He readjusted his glasses and spent the next few seconds looking about him, spying something darting in all directions around his head.

"What's wrong with you, Dad?"

"This flipping bee that has been making my life a literal misery!"

"Your actual life a misery? Really?"

"You know what I mean, child."

We began to walk towards the other two.

"You should be careful with Jared, you know. He's your brother, and you need to take care of him."

I scoffed at the thought. It was not as if I was killing the boy. Fine, we were fighting, but it was nothing serious.

"Dad, we were just playing. You sound like Mum. Weren't you like that when you were young with Uncle Pedro and Uncle Carlos?"

Dad often used to tell us all the stories of the three of them growing up. He used to tell Jared and I of the times he and the other two would be play-wrestling in their shared, Spanish bedroom in Alcobendas. Dad used to say that Uncle Carlos was the bulky one and eldest of the three. He, with his thick, black, shaggy hair and favourite Dennis the Menace, red and black T-shirt and black shorts, picked up a screaming, scrawny Uncle Pedro by the arms whilst Dad grabbed his jolting legs. Dad told of how they lifted and raised him high up to the delicately painted, cream white ceiling and pummelled the poor boy on to the thin deluxe mattress. Thing is, they brought Uncle Pedro down so hard that the wooden frame of the bed broke.

Nana was furious! He would giggle with the other two, when they were around for family parties, reminiscing about the way she would come with her tea towel, flamethrowing Spanish accusations and vehement at them, as they would duck and dodge about the house. Abuelo (that's 'granddad' in Spanish to you and me) chuckling in his rocking chair on the solitary veranda; basking in the warm, blazing sun and whispering breeze that swept about his dark, greying caterpillar moustache and wavering thick locks of hair.

"We were just playing. You, on the other hand, were not playing when he got that bruise under his rib!"

I dodged another yellow and blue Frisbee which zoomed past my head and was eventually caught by the jock in his red, back-placed cap.

"Well he shouldn't have…"

"He shouldn't have what? Taken the Xbox controller from you when playing that racing game?"

I knew that intonation in his voice. The way he said it made the whole scenario seem so base, so silly. As far as I was concerned though, it was the principle that mattered.

The thing is Jared and I never really got on. You would think that, as brothers, we would be close and would be there for each other. Unfortunately, we never seemed to get that bond. Dad would always tell us that 'family were supposed to stick together', but sometimes Jared was just so irritating.

Growing up was always a struggle with us two. I don't know whether it was the fact that we were both boys, and there was this alpha male symptomatic zeal going on between us, or whether we were just peas from different pods. The memory of him that really annoyed me the most was when he…

"Malachi, could you get the blankets from your dad please?"

Mum was in the business of protocol and procedure. She could never really rest even when the time was diarised to rest. She ushered us over with her hand, whilst Jared cast his eye across the beach, no doubt looking for some pretty girl to satisfy his new-found adolescence.

The wind was just right. The cool sensation that tickled across my cheeks and the calm billowing of the gentle waves of the sea, as I watched Mum carefully spread the blankets over the sand, could only make me think of one thing. I stared at my destination and took off my T-shirt, readjusting my shorts.

"I'm just going for a quick dip, Mum."

"Okay, be careful."

Dad giggled under his breath at the constant worrying of his dear wife, as he continued his husbandly duties of setting up the parasol; stabbing it into the sand and raising up the white sheets that cast a welcoming shade and shadow from the now beating, blazing sun.

And so my walk turned into a jog. My jog into a run. I could feel the wind whistle past my ears and cool down my already warming body. The air was swallowed interchangeably into my receiving lungs, as I panted across the hundred or so yards to the blue playing field that was filled with so many aquatic royalists. My toes scrunched as they formed a groove in the silky sand with each dash of my legs.

I could already taste the sea salt in the air, as I drew close enough to feel the changing texture under the soles of my feet from dry, gritty sand to slithering sludge. The water spat its flurry of aqua flies in the air, as my running turned into a scene from the 2012 Olympic equestrian try-outs; my legs hopping in and out of the ever rising water. The water was surprisingly warm. It blotted and dripped on my shorts; the cobalt colour turning into blueberry blue. The refreshing droplets of water on my face and chest filled me with a quick, snap judgment to leap up in the air. I lifted my arms above my head; the wind swiping through my legs for that brief second. I momentarily heard the laughter, the playful screams and the peripheral conversations. I squinted as the ember sunlight scorched through my eyes. I took in a deep breath; noting my increased heart juggling the blood around my body. Hands first, I hit the water that crashed around me; burying me, as I curved like a dolphin in the quintessential abyss that soon became my playground. As I opened my eyes, I noted all the multiracial, flapping array of legs above and around me; dancing in the open sea like a multitude of unsynchronised toy soldiers.

As the crowd of bubbles, big and small, ascended around me, I could just about hear the water-clogged noise that I once zoned into before I dove down here. I anchored my body lower, away from the surface, and swam about the dark green coral. As I let the waving seaweeds massage and tickle my abdomen and legs, I treaded the engulfing water to see the bug-eyed school of yellow-finned and blue-bodied fish mind their own orientation class; learning the ways of the water world.

It was so peaceful here. I swung around and noticed a twenty-centimetre wide, golden, orange and white, diamond-spotted starfish gliding through the watery highways without a care. As it curved its arms and waved each limb in my direction, I spotted a swarm of playful sand eels glimmering in the few darting rays of sunlight that cast their beam in the underwater sanctuary.

Darkness overshadowed the peaceful surroundings for a split second. But I hadn't blinked. A flash-like lighting cascaded around me and, in the flicker of a moment, I could swear that I could see for miles under the water at the lonely, black rocks covered in sticky, clingy algae, the extra-terrestrial-looking brittle star that spread across the universal ocean floor and the electric-blue, bobbing saucer jellyfish that planned on playing tricks on the heels and soles of so many boisterous fathers and sons.

The school of fish had instantaneously thrust themselves into the darkness. The sand eels had taken cover under the now cloud of dust on the sea floor; tails wagging as they burrowed and burrowed. As I looked up, I just about noticed the last pair of legs leave the sea, the ripples and waves of water being the only evidence of a once filled and enjoyed watery playground.

Suddenly, I was running out of breath.

I slapped my arms in the liquid jungle that had sheltered me from the recent, orbital flashed photograph and tipped my toes below me. I propelled myself towards the surface. My heart began to race. Was Mum okay?

I could feel the temples around my body pump and beat the increasing rate of blood around my body.

Dad?

I could feel the drumming in my ears, the tightening of my chest. Was I going to make it up to the top in time?

Jared?

My eyes enlarged, as my hands desperately clasped to be the first victors of the air I had once so freely breathed.

How long was I even down there for?

My eyes blurred. The surface couldn't be that far up. Maybe I had mistimed this whole affair. Maybe, this was it.

Of all the times in my life, I remembered my English teacher's favourite saying when we, the moaning class of high school students sought to petition against the reading of *Moby Dick*, "Now, now class, Jacques Cousteau once said that the sea, once it casts its spell, holds one in its net of wonder forever."

CHAPTER FOUR
The Key Maker

"Malachi?"

The call echoed through the hallway.

It sounded like Borus the key maker. His rough, hoarse voice raced across the stone walls and through to the vicinity of my room. The call woke me up from the flashback of a nightmare, and now I was back in my room. Sat up straight and perched like a crested crane in the African savannah, the bed sheets slithered down from around me, resting on my purple and green, striped pyjamas.

"Malachi!"

Slowly coming back to my senses, I could make out the jaundice yellow, stained-glass window effect at the top half of my warm, oak wood door that separated me from the hallway of this part of the property. The slabs of silver-grey stone across the rustic walls surrounded the room from top to bottom. The hollowing breeze of the wind that circulated through the fireplace in the left side of the room brought my attention to the two-metre window that gave sight to the majestic view of the Guild's grounds. I could see the brown and yellow, autumn-stricken leaves glide unwillingly across the view like a naughty schoolchild to the detention hall. I noticed, as always, the little race that took place of the green ivy stems that ascended from the bottom of the window seal on the outside. They would have, no doubt, begun their epic journey clinging to the Guild walls and shooting up the fifty or so feet up to my window where they could now stop and pose for my attention.

To my right, and next to the hollow, wooden stairs that led up to the bathroom, lay my own version of Excalibur: my sword. It was not called Excalibur. This is not a rendition of Merlin and King Arthur. It was just a sword. But not just any sword. A few months after the incident at the beach, the one whose name I would not even attempt to pronounce, it was given it to me. It stood proudly in its jet-black scabbard; the night-blue pommel clinging boldly on to its black coiled grip.

My sword rested on the heavy-footed, grand, mahogany desk whose splendid design and twirling features made it the centre of attention in the corner of the room. Upon it lay the only photo I had of my dad, mum, Jared and I. The picture was the first photo we took when we got out of my dad's silver Citroen Picasso at the beach that day. We looked so happy, as we stared at the camera which my dad held high above us all. Jared looked the silliest, pulling some funny face with his tongue out as he often did; always trying to be the one that everyone pointed and laughed at in a picture. Mum looked so rested and happy, as she smiled at the camera. Her eyes were, however, focused admiringly at her husband upon whom her arm embraced, behind me, who was in the centre of the photo. My dad, of course, with his supercool, black sunglasses on, pinged a reflection of the camera flashlight that went off as his thumb would have calmly pressed the shutter button.

Other than that, my quiver of arrows lay still on the surface of the table. The multitude of golden fletching led down to the sinew and brick-brown arrow shaft and disappeared into the encasing, fading, black pouch. My bow, on the other hand, gracefully encircled the container of arrows. The sturdy, pale-black string faced away from me, and the dark-brown frame and grip of the bow faced me, its owner, in silent servitude.

"Malachi!"

The drumming of Borus' voice spat my eyes into wide open vision, and I parted my mouth to shout out in response.

"Yes?"

The 'yes' came out like a croaking frog. You know the feeling of your throat when you have just woken up from a deep sleep and talking is not the first action your body had in mind, and it comes out all phlegmy and coarse? Yeah. That's how my response came out.

Bang, bang, bang.

The grand, one-metre-wide, wall-sized mirror that occupied the space between the table and the similar, wooden-bodied cabinet on its left wobbled slightly on the sturdy wall in response to the cataclysmic vibrations that interrupted its still stare back at the world.

The battering ram of Borus' fist on my door was the only confirmation I needed to know that this was not some sort of drill. Was it her? Now? I hadn't even got the eleme…

"Open the door, Malachi!"

Borus was never one for manners, but the constant banging that rung on the other side of my door was unusual for him.

"I'm coming! Let me just get changed."

I flung the thin, sky-blue sheets about me, as I scurried out of bed like an excited cat getting his feed. I tiptoed across the cold, stone floor and made my way to towards the four-drawer cabinet. Borus, however, had not stopped banging yet.

"Just one minute!"

I clasped the circular, iron handle from the first drawer, as a shook my pyjamas bottoms off. Whilst flicking off my pyjama bottoms to some random direction in the room, I opened up the first drawer and pulled out some underwear. Making my way to the second, I grabbed my black, denim trousers and struggled to put them on in the hurry that I was in.

"I'm going to just break this door down!"

By the time he had said that I was having my own personal issues in the midst of my chocolate-brown, hooded top. One arm was in the air, attempting to find the right hole, and my other arm was attempting to aid my eyes to see what was going on, as the brown, cotton fabric was all that I could view around me.

"Borus, you are a key maker. You don't have to break any door down."

The banging stopped.

Having stopped myself for a couple of seconds, I sighed – at last I had calmed Borus down. Having tied the last lace of my leather boots, I made my way to the door with a swanky, smug smile and reached for the golden latch and three locks that secured my door.

"You see, Borus. Waiting didn't kill you off, did it?"

I placed my hand on the cold, bronze handle and began to open the door.

"You are finished getting ready like woman now, eh?"

The familiar voice didn't come from in front of me, it came from behind. It was the same voice that had echoed me out of subconsciousness not so long ago. I turned around.

"Borus, what the…?"

Before I go any further, it is probably best to explain Borus.

Borus calls himself a key maker. He is the only one we know with the gift that he has and, by reason of the same, I can only presume that he is the sole person on earth with his kind of power. Borus stands at 6 feet and 5 inches tall – just a few inches taller than I – and he is built like (as we used to say back home) a house. His arms are probably the same width as my leg, and so I don't think he was joking when he said he would break my door down.

Borus originated from Leczyca, Poland. When I first met him, I remember him telling me off for thinking he was Russian. He would often reinforce his statement, time and time again, that he didn't like vodka and that their accents did not sound alike. As a new-born baby, he was left outside on a bus stop bench in the freezing cold, one lonely night, by his mother who was unable to take care of him, or so he was told. I was never quite sure why the answer to financial desperation would be to leave a child out in the unforgiving, cold Polish wind. He never talked about his past that much or how he came to the Guild. But what he did say was that the Guild was his home now.

He made his way to the table, authoritatively grabbed my sword and arrows and threw them in my direction. I grabbed them both and fastened them about me.

His shiny, white bald head was the first part of his body anyone noticed. It was probably because it was a rather big head. I could see the ripples of skin at the back of his neck, as he marched over to the table to grab my weapons. He was wearing his dark navy blue, double-breasted jacket. The night-blue, denim jeans that he wore led down to his heavy, leather, brown boots which resounded across the stone room, leaving wet marks in his path. The royal-blue and gold-tipped scabbard, which hung about his right hip, bounced as he paced. Borus had the insignia of a thick, medieval iron-style, silver key in the middle of the handle, and the brown, bow-shaped handle between the gold-tipped cross guards was the only tease you could see of his nugget-coloured, nine-inch blade of a dagger.

Where on earth had he been?

Literally.

The slight clinking of the zip at the top of each boot chimed in with the autonomous waving of his hairy, blonde arms. I could see the array of scars and cuts about his forearms from the many places he had travelled with some of the Elders in the past.

So yes… his gift.

Borus is able to create pathways and doors out of thin air. He carries a set of keys on his person that enable him to conjure up and create doorways to anywhere in the world and to here – where the Guild is. The clanging set of keys themselves are not exactly on show either. They are just as present as one's shadow. Even though you cannot see your shadow in the dark of night, it follows you like a ghost in a haunted mansion. What I mean is that you cannot always see the keys on him, but with a swift swipe of his hand he is able to manifest a key into his palm and shoot it into the air which opens up a veil of sorts into a whole new dimension. And that's how he got into my room. There is more to him, and his power, but that should do for now.

I had turned round just in time to notice the disappearing portal evaporate into thin air; the slight glimmer of light imploding in his tightly held fist as, no doubt, vanishing the key conjured there. As I did so, I noticed the brightly lit hallway outside my door. If only, in these three years that passed by, I would one day see my da…

"Jero has a mission for us. We must go now, Malachi."

He began to pace towards me with purpose and precision. The iridescent glimmer of the ten-inch knife on the left side of his hip grabbed my very brief attention. This particular knife was one that could do damage to any enemy or being that I could think of. The solid chromium handle circulated to the perfectly Borus-sized finger grooves at the bottom of the knife. Just above the finger grooves resided a sly chisel edge; the bridge between the index finger and thumb groove. This knife boasted a deep belly; the curved arc of the cutting edge. Jagged serrations swaggered at the tip of the blade; the top of the blade transforming to a darker chrome swage that contrasted to the somewhat flat spine of the knife.

My room was not exactly huge; on quick arithmetic, the room had a ten-metre length and a seven-metre width. I could see him checking off his mental list, as my questioning eyes met his solid, pale-blue eyes for a split second. He grabbed my left arm and turned away from me.

"Borus?"

The warm grasp around my forearm felt strong enough to stop the blood from flowing to my hand. I felt the jerk instantaneously take place in all of my muscles, as he tugged me forward, my eyes widening in communion with the sudden movement. He flicked his right hand in the air, as if he were flicking some sort of bug, and all of a sudden a rustic, rusty iron key appeared out of thin air in his hand.

"Borus. Not again!"

He cast his hand ahead of us, his index finger and middle finger facing the aerial target in the midst of the room, throwing the key forward. The key darted at bullet speed onward and, in an imploding white twinkle, dissolved into ripples about two metres ahead of us. The ripples cascaded from the single drop in the aerial pond, and as they violently simmered, the air tore.

It tore like a hand that had excitedly pierced though a wrapped gift, in the centre of the wrapping paper, and ripped from the centre outwards. As the portal door widened to its two-metre height and one-metre width, I could barely see anything. One was never able to hear anything that was going on on the other side of the portal, and the barely visible surroundings afar, past the portal, offset against some sort of building.

My heart began to race for first place, as my nutty-brown irises widened when I was within a step of going through the needle-thin curtain. Borus went through first; his pale white hand still resolutely gripped around mine. He looked as if he had just walked into a wall of water, as his body wavered into the nothingness of thin air momentarily. As he did so, I glared, in the slowness of time, at my still staring mirror, from whose point of view the portal was as thin as a paper; my dragged body its cinematic premier.

Borus silently disappeared in the blink of an eye.

"Borus, the last time I did this I was nearly siii…"

And in the next blink, I did too.

CHAPTER FIVE
Mission Meltdown

A playful gust of wind flurried around us. The hood of my top was tumbling in every direction in the brief cusp of wind and the tickling of the draft swayed through my clothes, face and hair, as I squinted through the whole escapade, while Borus continued his firm grip on my arm. That feeling of going down a speeding roller coaster is the only way I am able to describe the circus act that was taking place in my stomach.

"…icck."

In less than two seconds, the final curtain was called and the walk-through was over. It was, however, long enough to make me uncontrollably focus on the internal rumbling and tumbling of my internal organs, as our feet landed in a quadruple squish on the murky, muddy grasslands in the humid, sticky air.

"It was not so bad now was it, Malachi?"

In seeking to ignore his sarcasm, I clung to my stomach in order to somehow telepathically keep whatever was thinking of coming up… down. I could feel the moisture of the air penetrate down my trachea and into my lungs, as I took in my first breath of the foreign air. The whistling buzz of unknown flying insects joked about my ears, as I twitched my head repetitively. As I swiped about my ears, I felt the flapping disagreements of long, floppy leaves. The soft glide of the leaves upon my hand left a cool sensation, as the small droplets of the recent rainfall trickled down and through my fingers. The rest flickered about my hair and brow, causing me to blink and squint in the already hardly visible surroundings.

It was night-time, and the stars above, through the pitter-pattered gap of leaves, were twinkling in their millions like still fireflies in the heavens. The enormous, white moon sat peacefully in the universal silence above. The black and grey blotches, amidst the chalk-white ball, were shining beautifully.

"Where are we?" I asked eventually, having come to the conclusion that my internal organs had stopped salsa dancing.

"Matu." Borus did not even make eye contact; staring straight ahead. He cautiously stood a little bit in front of me to my right. If only he could see the contorted look of confusion on my face.

"Matu?" I replied, noting that Borus did not have any further plans to clarify where Matu actually was.

"Malaysia," Borus hoarsely whispered in a way that hinted that our location should have been blindingly obvious from the inception of our arrival.

"Malaysia!" I chocked back, raising my voice. "Why would Jer…?"

The palm of his huge, humid-ridden hand slapped the bottom half of my face, as he cusped my mouth and cheeks. My eyebrows took off a couple of levels above their normal position, as I felt the zing of blood seep through my palate and the bee sting (being my incisor teeth) that pierced my tongue. Borus held my head that tightly I could feel his charging pulse through his palm.

"Shh."

He lifted his index finger to his mouth, and he began to squat lower to the ground through the little woodland in which we found ourselves. As he did so, the stretching of my facial skin brought to light the commanding order to lower myself. Descending into crouching position, I simply continued to look in disbelief at the moonlight-reflecting, bald head.

It was only then that I noticed that Borus had not once looked at me since we'd arrived. His focus was transfixed on what was ahead of us. I felt a snail-paced wind trail through the widening gap between my mouth and his hand, as it transferred to the right side of his hip. In like-mindedness, I too looked ahead and, by reason of what I saw, I too instantaneously, yet carefully, latched on to the black grip of my sword.

*** *** *** *** ***

My screaming cry, in the wilderness about me, resounded in the crashing descent. In the dark, damp, dusty room under the curséd kampong was where I stopped tumbling down. I squinted in the limited moonlight, which slotted through the wooden floorboards above me. The cloudy fog of inhaled dust that juggled in the air around me caused me to cough and splutter, as it tickled through my throat and squinted water to my pained eyes. I could smell the earth that hovered about me; the sticky, irony of drought in my mouth being my only taste.

Having been cast down the sharp-edged stairs, like a bowling ball down an alleyway, by the dark, beast-like creatures (otherwise known as the Laden), most parts of my body were aching and in agony. I winced, as I sought to shift my weight on the rough, creaking floor, but the cramping contraction of my nerves in all of my muscles caused me to grimace at the pain of moving.

The floorboards above me creaked. I look up with expanded and side-switching pupils; the woeful wood contracted and bent, owing to the weight of the bodyguard above. The zigzag of the passing shadow across my face caused the pulse of my heart to increase and forced my blood through the internal highways at a heavier rate.

My long, muddy, brown hair had clumped and charged across my face due to the radiating, gummy moisture of the air and being cast down into the depths. The throbbing behind my eye sockets added insult to the ever growing list of injury.

I could feel the tight grip of the dry, prickly, rough rope around my blue, bloody wrists and legs hold me prisoner; wriggling either of them got me nowhere. The tenderness of my eggshell skin and battered chest made the very work of breathing a chore, as I lay there.

There was one part of my body that bore a definitive imprint; my left arm. The slick, muddy glare of the black handprint that gripped at the follicles was a very present warning of the reality of what we were up against.

*** *** *** *** ***

Through the blossoming thicket around us, I pierced my gaze across to the very beings that had kept the key maker tense in concentration.

A few metres ahead lay a swaying crowd of wheat and tares that glittered in the sallow moonlight above. The eerie breeze gave dark resilience to the haze in front of us that spanned the bumpy terrain that would end up soaking up the defeat of someone's final breath.

"We are going to need Harvey."

Speaking in his rascal-rough, European accent, Borus kept his eyes fixed on the prize that would see his damaging dagger become party to the proceedings. I didn't register the need to reply just yet; I could see through the verdant myriad ahead of us exactly why we would need Harvey.

There were at least seven of them that circulated around the haunted vicinity. The dark aura of the Grim Reaper surrounded each of them, fulfilling the ritual of death that sacrificed all prey who unfortunately stumbled into their wide path. The tips of their soiled, bone-white, Ankole-like horns were crowned with the red, blotched stains of their kill; the evidential topping over each sharp, bowed spear which I could easily distinguish in the pale effulgence on the marked battlefield. Their buffalo-style, animalistic, muscular definition blended in the strong, toned, human physique of these 7-foot tall, post-Olympic warriors. Clothed in the night blackness of their skintight, crude-oil fur; each muscle proudly defined these creatures from top to bottom.

What enchantingly invited fear into the nucleus of anyone's soul was the bronze glow that festered in their beastly faces.

Light is that which is supposed to dispel the darkness. Light is that which is to supposed to give sight to hope, and cast out trepidation, for those lost in the shadows. It is the magnetic glow of the candle flame that draws a moth to its fiery orbit. The two lights which embedded each Laden's head only shared one thing: the power to induce fear.

I could feel the blood flow to and from my heart harder and faster. The moisture in the curved walls of my mouth dried up like an Egyptian drought in the blazing heat of the day. I had to pull myself together.

My focus took the pedestrian crossing over to another one of the Laden who had sombrely appeared from the left corner of the kampong house.

"I will be back."

Borus carefully whispered the same, as he cast his hand diagonally to his right in a stern salute to the ground.

"Don't even zink about going at zhem alone."

"After 3 years of training, Borus, I think I can take…"

I turned around to my right side to notice the last wavering ripple of grass fall back into place as time seemed to have rewound the bomb blast that had once scattered the pieces of earth from each other.

Letting out a sigh of exasperated breath, I reached into my back pockets and pulled out my mud-brown, leather gloves; gliding them on to each hand to protect me from the cold and whatever else lurked ahead of me. From where I crouched in the darkness, the base of the kampong house floated on solid, wooden, rectangular stilts in the lush vegetation, which lifted the whole creation about two or three metres above the moist, mud-spattered ground. To the entrance of the timber castle, in the woodland, were the ten or so alluring steps which led to the veranda that tied itself to the perimeter of the dimly lit balcony. The regional, wooden patterns that made up the brackets in between the stairwell looked somewhat isolated; parts of the symmetrical design were compelled into second place, as the gaps in the linear equation proved that physical force had been the victor here.

This battleship looked a bit different to what I would typically expect from a traditional Malaysian house. I was able to see the other end of the mini savannah in between the logically set out wooden columns, but towards the right-hand side of the underside… a basement or some sort of container?

Through the tense atmosphere, the wind carried a sharp, cutting scream to my ears. It could have only originated from one direction.

I darted through the thin, thatched marsh towards the dark lair in the centre of the woodlands. Wading through the parting, long grass, I could feel the soft bristles of each thin, tango-dancing stem separate and tickle my face and hands. I briefly used them to elongate the line of vision, as I navigated through the vegetation towards the stairs.

I reached for my bow behind my back with my left hand and grasped, ever so discreetly, in symphony, with my right hand a bunch of arrows from the quiver that was securely strapped on my slightly damp back. My heart was thumping in my chest, and the vibrations resided in the bracket of my throat; the warnings and recommendations of Borus a ringing tinnitus in my mind.

Three arrows launched simultaneously into the air, with precision and purpose, from the marshy ground below. One of the gigantic Laden stood fearlessly by the entrance of the stairs, staring into the bracketed window of the house. In a tale of lumbering pace, the three, pointed warheads arched through the air like a rainbow and hailed a piercing end to their target; puncturing into the flesh of the beast. As the first stab entered into the centre of the warrior's lean and muscular, crude-oil back, the sting that damaged it makes it turn with bemusement and a slight wince. The second nick entered into the turning side of the Laden; it curiously seeking who dared to strike first.

The lumbering pace of time ended.

Its oval eyes flared with the fury of napalm, and its wide mouth parted to let out a roaring black hole of drooling saliva; like venomous, black ink. As it did so, it jabbed its hand violently in the consuming darkness, and in the flash of a moment, its weapon appeared. The like-minded dark, double-bladed battle-axe, joined together by the blood-dripped, silver, slicing spear, appeared. The foot-long, twin-sharpened blade on each side of the handle curved symmetrically in the pale moonlight. The archaic point of the blade, which invertedly hooked in the middle of the cutting edge itself, led to the crusted, dark-brown, Grim Reaper claw that held the family of blades together. The night-black, thick pole was bridged together by a foot-long strip of what looked like metallic chain. It began to swing the axe in a hurricane of animalistic anger.

The third arrow forcefully glided through the boulder of its neck causing it to stumble backwards and choke. As it staggered back, the mini earthquake alerted the other three or four Laden that something was not right. Drips of black mess oozed over the shaft of the penetrator.

I jumped metres high, up into the air, in silent courage, my frame casting a silhouette in the moonlight; the blades of grass and flickers of mud pirouetting around me in the soft tune of the wind. I swayed above the laddered stairs, as a pianist would ascend from octave to octave. With my bow straddled about my back again, my hands reached for the cool sheath where my sword was harboured. With elegance, the peal of my sword stripped through the air, as the silver blade reflected the ashen light like a beacon of effervescent hope.

The ancient, thin, sprawled, black lines across the central, navy-blue fuller could be boldly seen, and the blade itself became jagged as you approached the base. It imitated the anatomy of a dragon; the sharp neck and piercing head being the blade and the horn, nailed wings being the lower body of the silver blade. The talons of the dragon's feet were mimicked as you reached the sturdy metal cross guard, the sides of which split into the protectively intelligent, antennae-like claws about the edge of the sword.

Against these creatures, I was going to take no chances. It was time to tap into the sword's power, from the onset, against the Laden on my own; even if it would drain my power and energy that bit quicker.

"Tempus[1]!"

I shouted with the valour that pumped through my veins, as my eyes locked into the fiery furnace of the wild Laden that had now broken the shaft of the arrow in its neck and cast it on to the veranda. The black lines glowed solidly in the darkness of the night and changed to an icy blue, as the personality of my sword changed at my command. The once silver, smooth body of the blade manifested into a golden cutting edge, as the rhapsody of its chime echoed in the gravity of its bright glow.

The descent began, and as I landed, I swiped my hands through the air with all my force, gripping my sword in its shimmering bravado, and came down upon the neck of the Laden. The blade barely sliced through the muscular column. I paused for a millisecond of disbelief, as I took anxious puffs of air with wide eyes darting from the injection made by my sword to the heated glare in the eyes of the Laden. I noticed it swing its battle-axe for my head, and I wrenched the sword from its neck, turning around clockwise whilst descending at the same time, swooping my sword at its legs. The battle-axe just missed taking off my forehead, as the gust of strong wind blasted past the top of

---

1 Time

59

my head. As my sword cut into the Achilles tendon of the Laden, it roared in (what I would hope to assume was) pain and violently kicked me in the midriff across the splintered veranda with its free right foot.

The unwanted exile of air blasted from my lungs, as I slid and tumbled like a rag doll across the floor; my hand clutching desperately to my sword. The joints in my body connected and made a drum roll in the orchestrated fight that I'd initiated. The Laden began to run at me.

Well, I say run. Tempus had taken its toll on the Laden with the two strikes already made. This would put me at some advantage. As I postponed the current daze and ache from my body, I rose; skipping up on to my feet and swiping the shards of dust and splinters across my forehead with my free left hand.

As the Laden stomped towards me – slower than it usually would have done had I not used my sword's special ability – swinging its axe again in the flurry of the air, I too charged. It swung for the bottom of my legs, but I remembered the one capoeira move that I was taught when I learnt how to fight: the aú giro sem mão. I jumped off with my right leg into the air; my opposite arm driven around and towards my chest in order to create enough torque to rotate towards the horned reaper before me. The twin blade of the axe this time must have at least swiped a few strands of my moist hair, as my eyes clocked it swimming underneath me like a shark gasping for blood.

My foot, cased in its hard-soled boot struck hard in the middle of the Laden's head. It consecutively jerked out a splatter of thick, black, oily liquid on to the ground from its mouth. My right hand, sword in tow, followed the attack with a commanding pummel into the back of the bowing Laden like the sword in the stone; the first third of the blade of my sword slicing out of its torso,. The Laden crashed on to its knees. As I pulled out the sword with my right hand, I clenched my fist, swung around and uppercut the Laden with my left, which elevated the beast into an involuntary hover in the air. I clasped my sword again and swung it from the floor up to cleanly slice the Laden from its groin to its tightened chin. Its black blood splattered into the atmosphere, as the splodges gathered upon the rotting ceiling of the kampong veranda. My right leg sprang into action, as I finally straight kicked the Laden, in its stomach, across the veranda, pushing from my hips to gain greater extension. The enemy crashed to the floor once and for all; the candle of its eyes blowing out in the wind.

The recent hustle and bustle had now alerted the attention of the other Laden about the perimeter. As my chest inflated and deflated above normal capacity, I could feel the bolting vibrations through my hot feet. Something or some things were coming up behind me.

"Whoa!"

I turned in the fraction of time to notice a clenched, cannon of a fist aiming for my marvelled face. The gunpowder of fire was seen in the seething eyes of the marksman. With wide eyes and bated breath, I swooped down quickly and gambolled under the parted legs of the Laden.

As I tucked under the steaming, black fury whose blow I had just escaped, I stabbed my sword into the giant oar of the Laden's foot. I was too awkwardly placed at the time, as my neck flattened upon the timber veranda. I heard the sharp shout of agony engulf the air. I pivoted on my knee and flicked my head back to notice the Laden focus its horns towards the still sword which was dripping with a symphony of black and gold. It grunted grievously as it vehemently tugged the sword out of its stone, and threw it across, behind it, over the wonky, wooden banister; out of sight.

I stared like a hawk hopelessly, as I saw the last golden, rotating glimmer disappear over the edge of the veranda. As the wind continued to navigate through the thick follicles of my clumped hair, I could taste the stale lump of crude blood that must have sailed on to my lips from the previous warrior. As I turned back to face the raging buffalo, I saw it walk powerfully at me with full assurance of confidence in victory; not giving away any sign of physical ailment from the wound I had so recently inflicted.

My heart once again began to sound the ricochet of alarm bells though my sore body. My neck tilted higher and higher; the ripples in my forehead increasing as the Laden trudged forward. The internal scroll of contingency plans was getting shorter and shorter with every passing shudder of the ground it stomped on. I had to do something!

The soreness of my belly made me wince slightly, as I briefly flashbacked to the author of its existence. Now was not the time to show pain in my body language. As I rose, the Laden flicked its right, rough hand, pumping its arm like a shotgun, its battle-axe flashed into existence like a power-up in a computer game. It's two eyeballs of fire never glared elsewhere but upon me, as it let out an evil grunt of laughter; the black hole opening to reveal the placid waterfall of foam around it, each drop dripping upon its ragged fur and the floor. The face-flinching grind of the blade that scuffled on the floor was a distinctly unpleasant sound. Finally, it swung.

I flipped back in instinctive reaction. My hands took my weight momentarily on the now slightly bent kampong wooden floor, as I pumped myself up off the ground and on to my feet. The left clenched cannon fired for me again. This time, I was the one who was too slow.

In a flurry of quick motion, my head was unwillingly shot to the left. The blast that exploded through my right cheek, and into my head, lit up a cluster of fireworks in my nervous system. The world waltzed around me, as I could feel the weightlessness of the air propel me backwards and away from the Laden. The air played about my body; the hood of my top flopped about the back of my head, soaking up, no doubt, the speckled droplets of blood that my palate instantaneously had the displeasure of tasting.

I felt the full rejection of the solid barricade of a wall that cemented my aerodynamic body of its feeble state, the sort of feeling a pigeon would undergo when it made the humorous connection with your car windscreen as you mind your own business towards your destination. The multiplied set of birthday beatings you got from the handful of testosterone-filled lads in the rugby team. The crushing full stop gave gravity the opportunity to do her work and dropped me to the hard floorboards.

I landed heavily on my side. The reverberating throb repeatedly resounded through my head, my cheek began to swell slightly, as the adrenaline anxiously worked its way around my body; seeking silently to distract me from the depths of physical agony I should be feeling. The Laden was too close to shoot with my bow and arrow. In any event, judging from the proximity of space between the Laden and I, doing so was relatively futile. I slid myself on to my bum; my back resting on the hard wooden wall that had halted my airborne flight. My legs sprawled somewhat helplessly in front of me like a mini version of the river Nile; my whole body gasping to take in extra amounts of oxygen to contemplate survival. Every part of me ached. The bitter taste of a fight was the very reality that someone was going to get hurt, or even die.

The countdown of the battleaxe started. In the curtain calling, fluttering of my eyelids, I just about saw that it began to close the four-metre divide between us. I lifted my shaking arm up in front of me; ignoring the pinpricking pain in my limb as I did so. My palm was stretched out facing down towards the impending gladiator. My locked arm began to tense as the call started. I could make out the slight indentations of my fingers protruding from my gloves; my will blocking out the continual tang of the mixed cocktail of blood and saliva.

Three metres.

Awaken o sword of my valour!

Perhaps Borus was right. Perhaps I should have waited. Perhaps I should not have acted like a hormonal teenager and met his learned advice with an unlearned repertoire of childish cynicism.

Two metres.

Borus and Harvey should have been here by now! What was taking them so long? All Borus simply had to do was teleport there and back. It was not like he needed to go through airport customs! Come on!

One metre.

"Aargh!"

My arm was still stretched out towards the Laden. It must be thinking that I was reaching out for help; for sympathy; for mercy. The strain was taking its toll on my arm now. The sort of feeling you get when you are far too enthusiastic for an hour in class, rocketing your arm up into the air with wide eyes, wondering why on earth the seemingly blind teacher was not clocking your obvious desperation.

Its axe gathered speed; the friction from the splintered floor screeching momentarily until it rose into the air behind the Laden. Why wasn't my sword...?

*** *** *** *** ***

And then I heard it. The guillotine of death had imbedded the wood above; casting the mortal chasm between the two parts of the body that were once upon a time one. The male's war cry that had once given me hope had now echoed into a distant crescendo.

No standing ovation.

No round of applause.

Just silence.

Just the cold, lucid light that crackled though the floor above and the claustrophobic comfort of darkness that autonomously hugged me.

Whoever he was, he was now dead.

CHAPTER SIX
Above the Surface

Life had never been characterised so clearly like the first implosion of air that filled my burning lungs, as I crashed through the clear, liquid glass and into the open atmosphere. The gulp, splutter and choke combination played in confused collaboration, as I treaded the water, seeking to stay afloat.

The commotion around me painted too blurry a picture for me to focus on. I resurrected from the water facing in between the vast ocean and the beach itself. My hair was clinging to my brow like a stubborn, sticky lollipop; the sauna in my diaphragm a present source of heat in the now ghastly weather.

The barrage of discombobulated noise was crashing into my ears from all directions. I could barely focus on the aerial traffic that blocked out the internal voice of cognition and reasoning in my head.

My family.

I turned with mouth wide open. The salty splashes of the sea jumped in and out of my mouth in the crazy circus around me. I spat out the same in subconscious reaction, as my limbs kicked into action. I torpedo my way towards the beach those many of yards in front of me.

I paused for want of breath and treaded the water again. I wiped my face and eyes with my right hand in an attempt to offer the olive branch of visual clarity towards the once sun-kissed, sandy shore. The malarkey of madness was having her wicked way. Her hypnotising scent was wading through the crowds. Mothers clung to children with protective force, as toddlers fumbled up and down. Glancing to the left, one child wailed with arms blasted forwards towards the sandy surface; its red, toy truck barely visible to him now, as the sprinkles of sand, that were cast above it, sealed it into its new grave. The concerned father was staring into the atmosphere, as he pardoned his way through the crowd looking for, perhaps, the rest of his family tree that had been uprooted from him in the stampede of human rhinos.

My eyes darted left and right across the sandy plain. I was unable to see Dad, or Mum or Jared. Wouldn't they have tried to look for me? Why weren't they peering in worried stature, with hands clapped about their mouths and looking out to sea for me? I flashed back to Mum taking such care of Jared shortly after our little squabble.

No.

She wouldn't have been that mad to even contemplate leaving me here in some sort of justified chastisement.

Dad?

The strings of my heart had begun to play a sore, sombre ensemble, as I took a deep breath and beat against the waves to shore. I remembered the drive to the beach from home.

*** *** *** *** ***

We had left rather early before dawn and Mum, who was sat in the front passenger seat, and Jared, sat behind Dad, had fallen asleep;

Jared's head routinely attempting not to fall off that sturdy neck of his.

"You must always remember your family, Malachi," Dad said softly with both hands on the steering wheel; the thick brown hair protruding from his forearms which eloped from his white shirt.

"Did you hear me, Malachi?"

Dad's eyes' attention briefly crossed from the road to the rear-view mirror; his paternal brown eyes residing in my soul.

"Yeah I know, Dad." I sighed; trying to avert his gaze and look out of the clear window into the dizzying, passing woodland from the silver surfer we were cruising in. The droplets of sunlight had not begun to attempt to break through yet; the sun still storing his energy under the cloudy duvet.

"My mother. She was everything to me. She had often told me the same thing, and I would pull the same expression as you did."

I could feel his soft gaze upon my face. My eyes shifted from the outside to the inside; my own gaze now falling upon my thighs, my fumbling fingers anxiously cascading over each other.

"You know, son. It was only after I lost her that I realised how precious family actually is. And then…"

He paused for a moment and concentrated on the hypnotising rectangular lines that repetitively dove under the car.

"The way she was taken from me. From us…"

"Dad…"

"Son. Do not let hindsight be the teacher of your life."

Jared snorted and licked his lips like a lizard; shifting his weight from his neck to his right elbow that perched on the somewhat slippery windowsill.

"If I could just ring her one more time to tell her that I loved her."

His eyes shifted back to the winding road; his wrist rising slightly into the air, as the steering wheel sailed to the left. The smooth anchoring of the car to the body caused a monotonous swaying on this long journey.

"*I miss her too.*"

"*My mum always used to say that I should always tell my brothers that I loved them.*" *He chuckled in personal memoir.* "*Your Uncle Carlos? Hah! We spent most of our memorable youth as enemies!*"

Dad set his right hand on the wheel and used his left as an illustrative guide.

"*The arguing; the fights; the revenge. Ack! When you get older and look back, all those things are such rubbish. You look back and realise that the things you argued about and were passionate about fighting for are completely irrelevant.*"

As he spoke, I sought to gather my best arguments to rebut what he was saying. All the instances in my life where I was right and Jared was wrong flashed before me like a projected film on a wall. My moot points were ready!

"*Dad, Jared is a completely different person when you and Mum…*"

"*Malachi, when you were much younger; when Nana died. I know I was in a bad place, but that did not mean that I did not notice what was going on around me.*"

His calm eyes met mine, as I glanced up from my tensed legs to the rear-view mirror.

We both entered into simultaneous flashbacks.

"*I never neglected to notice the times you would keep Jared distracted upstairs, or in the other room; playing a board game or telling him to play hide-and-seek somewhere else so not to see me sad.*

"*Just remember that I am proud of you, Malachi. I am proud of the young man that you are growing up to be. But do listen to my advice. Look out for Jared; just like I will always look out for you.*"

*** *** *** *** ***

69

"Dad?"

The forceful push of the waves behind me slapped my head with the pressure of cold force. While my face was splattered with water, a new stream had flowed down my cheek, as my eyes welled in the concoction of fear and desperation.

"Dad!"

My cry got lost in the barricading cackle of the thunder that battered sound waves into my shadowed spirit. The sky's temper began to rage. The aggravation of billowing clouds above me swirled in scowls of black, grey and red, flashing in the photographs of the sky. I looked to where the sun once sat proud; where it had sat in the clear blue parchment up above a smiling community of fluttering beach butterflies.

What looked like the moon had now sneaked in front of the great ball of fire. The blazing glory of the sun had lined the perimeter of the galactic sphere that had plunged the world around me into cinematic darkness.

Something wasn't right.

No, I was very aware that something wasn't right a long time ago! I did not need a flashing, blood-red sky and slapping waves, culminating into a low-lit lair of a world to conclude that all was not as it should be.

What was this eclipse doing here?

Jared, with his random knowledge of science, had once said that the proximity of the moon affects the magnetic impulse of the waves, but this was something else! Wading through the now shallow water, I knew that whatever science experiment we were under, what was happening was becoming ridiculous! An eclipse was not due for another ten months. How did I know? Because the eclipse was supposed to take place on my birthday… in April. And even if, on the unlikely balance of lady luck's probability, I'd just got it wrong, the weather herself was riddled with hormonal malevolence.

I cascaded on to the beach like a newborn fawn trying to find the sturdiness in its young, feeble and shaking legs for the very first time. The cold pinch of the wind bit around my body. The sludge of sand buckled around my prune-like toes; the once soft sand garden was now a waterlogged marsh of bark-brown grit. My blue shorts were cascading heavily with water. Where was everybody?

The once calm firmament… I could just about make out distorted faces twisting in pain; the clouds screaming down at the earth in wrath. The soot-black blanket of the devil was clearly a catalyst to the intermittent screams and shouts from the far-distant cluster of civilisation, busting into getaway cars in the distance; the black, red, silver and miscellaneous dots driving into invisibility.

Where was my dad?

I coughed and spluttered the salty saliva that nearly crept down my throat, as I inhaled and exhaled deeply, eyes wide open in frowned despair, my nose running with all sorts of liquid mess, as I sniffed in the cold air. All this time, I had negated to consider the possible reason why the cool crowd had left the vicinity like scattered sheep in response to the growling pack of wolves.

I turned around.

My heart.

The bass strummed harder and harder.

I became more aware of the escalation of my breathing. The fight or flight option of my brain had been frozen in both time and space.

Have you ever seen rain fall on a naked power station? The naive sky dwellers that parachute, in their billions, upon the earth. The gentle hum of the pylon column silently crackling the wayward droplet as it sizzled in a spark of evaporation; its millions of comrades meeting the same end. On the cusp of the horizon, out at sea, that is what I saw in the growing darkness. The numerous dotted, raindrop sparks that filled the void like bronze fireworks.

The wolf whistle of the whispering wind soothed past my frigid ears. I clocked that I was presently the only one on the beach.

Alone in the nightmare.

Perhaps what happened was that I had actually drowned. I was just unconscious at the moment. All this was just a bad dream in limbo. I would just wait for the last gust of wind to take hold of my lungs and wake up to a crowd of faces around me; all worried and concerned-looking, with pale eyes and hands upon chests in relief, as I would rise from the sandy shore, splurging all manner of liquid in quiet thanks; the hard part of the back forcing the last rivers of death from my lungs.

I double took a reluctant glance to my right and noticed a breath of fog protruding; the grey Casper flowing like a ghost in my direction; its wings spanning the width of the once foot-piercing, hot beach and into the crashing, dark, foaming waves. The large pack of flickering lights coming from the horizon commanded my intermittent attention. That was until I heard the crisp war cries from the direction of those bronze candles in the windy distance.

The wallowing descent of dread killed courage in the soul of a young lion, as the predecessor of the pride pranced in the savannah plain and roared in authority. And I was all alone.

Hugging myself with shivering hands, as the distant sparklers got brighter and bigger with each little step I took back, my heels grovelled into the slimy sludge. I looked up to the sky for remorse; seeking to force out a prayer to the heavens as I know Mum would have me do, but the heavens had already turned into hell's menacing vehemence. The flick of dainty hail that pinged off my nose was the only response I received.

As I shook my head in shock at the foul ball that sprung from above, I woke up to the realisation that the thick blanket of fog had covered everywhere around me. However, unlike the warming embrace of the feathered duvet about your body as you cling to cosiness and snuggle into the comforting night, the cloudy mist filled me only with uncertainty and vulnerability.

I ran.

"Just remember that I'm proud of you, Malachi."

I just ran.

"I'm proud of the young man that you are growing up to be…"

I didn't even know what direction I was running in, but I did not want to wait for the consequences to catch up with me.

"But do listen to my advice."

My lungs burned, as the cold air swept into the corners of my chest. My diaphragm raised and lowered ever the faster; my naked feet flicking clumps of sand into the air like a trench that had just been mortared. Each hand just reached in front of my face, as they pummelled back and forth in the race for my life.

"Look out for Jared; just like…"

I just ran. Against my will, I entered into the fog, instead of me snuggling into the warmth of the duvet…

"…I will always look out for…"

The sly shadow of mystic darkness covered a scared teenage boy alone.

"…You."

Alone in the wilderness.

CHAPTER SEVEN
Flashback

Shooting up like a jack-in-the-box from the smouldering duvet left me dripping and crowded in trickling sweat. Blasting my eyes into the silent darkness was another continual effect of that day.

A twig knocked on the window. The eerie finger prodded on the thick glass; its shadow protruding as a magnified monster, the moonlight's ray cascading like a laser throughout.

The cloak of sweat clothed me in sticky fabric. The deep huff and puff racing from my lungs filled the void that the repetitive tick-tock of the circular clock in the room echoed... echoed... echoed. All my weight was on my hands that were spread like pancakes behind me; arm stretched out as if I were held back by some form of dark, invisible rope.

The soft, silky sheet of the white duvet lay crumpled about my legs. The silver trail of embroidery about the edges could barely be made out. The temperature changed in the solitary pit where my knees to my feet lay.

From sand to silk, my feet had not been aware of such a feeling of comfort for quite a while. Looking up at the ceiling, I was met only with the stone-cold stare of the black void of galactic darkness; the pitter-patter of light spot danced about the room like distant stars in the heavens. I remembered the billowing clouds that...

The smell of the dripping liquid about my body signalled that I was in need of a refreshing shower. In the robe of the night, I could feel the moist stickiness of my sheets where I lay, as if the very raindrops that had splattered around me in my nightmare had somehow teleported into reality.

I was very aware of my breathing. The particles of memories flickered and faded before my eyes. As a tear rolled down my cheek, the individual stream within the river created its own way. I heard the crashing rain outside the thick window which separated me from the vast outside. The darkness was very able to make one claustrophobic.

I closed my eyes, scrunching my eyelids shut together; the grimace of my face crumpled up my mouth like a worn-out newspaper. I tried to forget. Tried to ignore and black out the scene of the power station that flicked fireworks in the distance. I attempted to lower the volume of the loudening cries coming from the horizon. I clenched my toes; just like I would have done when each footstep would meet the sludge of sand beneath, hoping to take flight into a scene of sobriety.

I kicked off the duvet from my feet; the whoosh of air sweeping though my toes and about my calves, combating the clutching fabric of my purple and green pyjama bottoms that could barely be seen in the stripy light from the white ghost in the sky. The piercing bite of the freezing stone floor forced me to tiptoe in the darkness. The muscles in my legs felt fatigued from the fartlek they had endured in visions gone by. Two worlds converged into one when my mind wandered back to the moment I…

"Argh!"

I thunderously thumped my toe on the tricky, trespassing leg of the room's table. The throbbing creaks channelled through the atoms of my first three toes and transcend alarm signals to my brain. If anything were to attempt to wake me up, it was that. I gritted my teeth in agony. Times were hard enough as it was. The lack of comfort betwixt the pins and needles in my feet brought me down another level.

The pale light of the moon that flutteringly floated into my room guided me to the first step of the escalating stairs. I was running on 'middle of the night' autopilot and was all the more thankful for the gentle assistance of Mother Nature to my vision.

The limpness of my limbs commanded the frail collection to suddenly move my left hand, as I swooped towards the wall. I failed to lift off in time and the blockade of stone met the intersection of my shoulder and forearm. My head rested briefly on the vertical stone pillow; my eyes flapping like a dying bird.

Up another.

Ascending to the top of the stairs was nothing short of a tedious affair.

Before I could consciously compute, I was at the top of the stairs. I leaned, rather lazily, to the right and my body connected with the responding bathroom door. The obedient glide of the wooden frame on its bronze hinges swept a gust of bleached air into my nostrils. The clean smell of lemon and lavender transcended though my nasal passages, causing me to forget the so recent shadow of sweat that had gripped me in both fear and sadness. The crystallised, dark-grey floor continued to feature in this room. I could just about make out the anatomy of the surroundings.

My hand clasped in the air for the brown string that would transform the dark, citrus smelling room into light. I then felt the hanging, thin rope fly away in response to my most recent grab for vision. I noted the pendulum swing and caught the thin, textured string in my hand and gently pulled it down slowly like a steam train driver.

The burst of vision hit my eyes, as the particles of the room merged together in the dimming of my pupils. The tooth-white glistening of the toilet to my right, in the four by three-metre room, was the first object that grabbed my attention. The toilet seat was always down. After years of Dad slapping the back of my head for leaving it up because "germs were escaping into the atmosphere", it had to be down.

Dad…

The dainty, wooden cabinet sat comfortably about a metre above the rectangular toilet tank; the two doors split by the partition in the middle of it were closed. The little brown knobs were the simple ticket into the inside where four shelves lay that were no longer than my forearm.

I took a step forward and the tip of my toes on my left foot felt the comforting cuddle of the cotton fabric of the bath mat.

I placed my hands on the solid sink. Its oval anatomy gave it the ability to bounce its ivory complexion about the bathroom. With my head bowed down, I counted the fingers on each hand, as they played some clustered tune on the imaginary piano, gripping a crescendo with the invisible choir behind me. The silver surface of the posh, plated tap was a central masterpiece. The long neck stretched forth from the body of the sink; the four pronged hands on either side poking out like oval balloons. The metallic stopper was placed notably around the stem of the tap.

My left hand rose, and the whistling of the pipe gave precedence to the quiet hush of the clear water which descended from the tap. Like a caring mother to a baby, I cusped my hands together and held them momentarily under the mouth of the mini waterfall. The cool sensation penetrated through my nerves, as the puddle of water in my hands began to quietly overflow. I never really took the time to notice such things, but this time I studied my hands.

I studied the dark-brown lines that the Great Architect above had given me (whilst He fearfully and wonderfully knitted me together in the womb) through the rippling pool that had manifested in the cup of my hands. Carefully manoeuvring my fingers back and forth, I created designs in the creases of my parchment...

Dad, when I was younger, used to lie next to me when I was tucked in my bed with a return ticket to the land of dreams. He would place my tiny hands in his fully grown and warm, big hands and play games with me; seeing who would spot the similarities or differences first in the ancestral line. His finger would lovingly dance and draw over the various tracks of my hands, telling me some old folk story of how many children I would have because I had so many lines on this or that finger; the slightly ticklish sensation leaving a transparent snail trail over each groove.

A blink merged my dad's paternal instincts with time and space, and I suddenly realised that I was running a trail in my hand with my own finger.

I fluttered my hands down to cause a dam-breaking cascade of water around the inside of the sink. Some splashes found themselves elevated and rocketed on to the egg-shaped, one-metre tall mirror in front of my face. I closed my eyes in telepathic response to the contraction of my biceps. I bowed my head over the sink and encountered a momentary bliss of water over my face. If only I could wash away the thoughts of…

"I will always look out for…"

A second blast of water hit my face. The intruding prints of my fingers could be felt lightly pressing about my face and skin, as I wiped and extracted the sandy sleep dust from my weary eyes.

I was staring at the young man in the mirror. He looked tired; glum. His dark, mahogany eyes were surrounded by a scarlet arena. He stared right back into the windows of my soul; suspended in both space and time.

The playful clusters of rain drops slid down his face. His hair spiked in all directions like a mad troll. He smooths it down in a swift motion, breathed out a sigh and released the grip on the ivory sink.

Ahead of me now, and to the left, was the bone-white bathtub. The little ship cocooned at the back of the bathroom was my destination to get rid of the smell of perspiration. I pushed down and slid off my elastic-banded, stripy pyjamas and kicked them to the side under the S-shaped towel rail on the left wall.

I slid the turnstile and the showerhead burst forth, massaging streams of water that sprinkled and splattered all over my body. The mountainous goosebumps, that had routed valleys on my skin, had now abated under the liquid radiator.

The small bathroom soon picked up steam. The invisible heat molecules transformed themselves into a misty shadow. One eye squinted towards the mirror, and the condensation had left a silver-grey veil over the reflection of the young man. The soothing smell of soap soon swam across my nostrils.

As I turned, the blanket of steam billowed in the thickening surroundings; clouds of white froth folded in on themselves as I turned. I was but a moth in a humid swamp. I took a deep breath, and I could taste the fog melting on my taste buds. The fog cast a surreal sheet over anything in front of me.

How far was I going to run alone in the belly of the ghost?

*** *** *** *** ***

The crackling cackle of the thunder beat down on the drums in my ears. Vibrations of the sound stuttered making me knock-kneed. The cotton cloud failed to catch me and I fell onto the sandy shore.

The splatter of my body on the ground, under the aerial dam, had cast a grenade of thick, brown mud on my face. My right hand reached through obligation to wipe the grit out of the creases in my eyes but offered no great assistance.

A flashback of Mum fussing over Jared blinked through my eyes.

Unforgiving rain mortar-blasted sandy shrapnel around my body, and I could see the grooves where my body once lay, as I slowly attempted to pick myself up. Completely dumbfounded for words and all alone, I lifted my hands to my eyes to watch the painting wash away on to the floor. The flash photographer in the sky sent jagged arrows of blue and ice-white light; shooting his pointed tail in the heavenly dynasty.

The wind echoed past me. Echoed as it rode like a chariot, the cloud about me, and drew my attention to its focused direction.

The implosion of a tiny star bloomed nearby. The signal sparkled my attention, and I found myself magnetised, drawn towards it, as if some earthly black hole had formed. Casper, with no credence to the brushing apart by the wind nor the hovering of the sparkling diamond, began to fade and, instead, as I approached the spiralling fairy lights with hand before face, formed an arena around me.

"Malachi?"

The soft sooth of the voice graced a mysterious warmth in the arctic surroundings and, as if born of the light, three figures stood before me.

What on earth was this?

I couldn't believe my eyes. The army of droplets continued to hammer down upon the sand but not upon us. It seemed that the aura of these... people had not only caused the fog to encircle us but also caused the bleating and battering hail and rainfall to create a curtain about us. This was all a startling reminder that not everything was as it should be.

Who were these people?

I beheld these men as one would study a painting from afar in a museum.

Where did they come from?

The first man on the left looked the youngest out of the three. His fresh-faced skin, in my view, was a giveaway – late twenties perhaps? Even in the murky and dotted light about us, I noted his leather-black hair that was cleanly cut about his head and clean-shaven, eggshell-coloured face. Earthly, brown eyes shot in my direction and broke past the window to my soul, and somehow left me feeling both safe and worried at the same time.

His calm and youthful composure was reflected in the clothes he was wearing. A plain white T-shirt that showed off his lean, muscular build sat on his shoulders. About him was flung an oak-brown cloak that was held silently and confidently by a majestic cloak pin; its silver surface glimmering in its own reflection. From where I stood, it looked like the face of a pocket watch without the surface. Everything was laced in silver. Each dial stood proud; flowing from a path of the outer circle of the signet. It was the same metallic face that sat in front of his waist, his belt no doubt securing the navy-blue trousers that he was wearing, which eventually lay scuffled around his night-black, leather shoes that looked like hiking boots. Poking out of his right side was...

Am I dead?

I think... a sword? A real sword! I didn't know, but I dared scarcely take my eyes off him, not the golden-laced, red scabbard that poked its head from under this man's cloak.

Or am I going to die?

My toes clenched the soft, slushy sand beneath just to make me feel like I was holding on to something, like I was being comforted by something or someone else rather than the children of the chill that were feasting on the goosebumps of my shivering skin. The drip dropping symphony of the seawater from my shorts reminded me that it wasn't too long ago that they were dry. That it wasn't too long ago that I had tasted the melting rays of the sun. That it was not too long ago that they were being tugged on by my younger brother, Jared.

Jared.

Are these angels?

As I took a step back, arms cuddling me in both directions, I felt the laser pointer stare of the middle man. In the dark, pale light of the night my attention was drawn straight away to the slicing scar in his cheek. The wound affirmed its position in the midst of his golden-blonde, cotton beard. He stood with one arm to his side; the one leading to the hand that held the bold, black staff that dug its heel into the ground. The tip of the staff was succinctly golden, and although we were shrouded in mist and hail, it shone so brightly, as if the sun's rays had pummelled though the fog just to reach her target. His emerald-green eyes matched the bold cloak he was wearing over his shoulders that was clasped together by a similar cloak pin. He wore a brown, long-sleeved shirt that was comfortably baggy about his torso. His black trousers matched the invisibility of the night over his similar leather boots that made a trench in the sand where he stood.

Am I dreaming or unconscious?

The well in my eyes rose to the surface. The chill of the night had forced a scuffle in my breath, as I longed for the warm embrace of my father. Perhaps I would see Nana shortly when these three mercenaries were done with me. The supernatural paralysation held me in fear, and the stuttering pulse of my breathing was lost in the wind.

The third man at the end was most certainly the eldest and the wisest-looking of the three. My grandfather always used to say that "with age, comes wisdom". Now if that were the case, this man was definitely the wisest of them all. He didn't have any visible weapon that I could see, but the aura about him played a magical chorus in the atmosphere surrounding him.

Am I in the twilight zone?

A bold, blue cloak rested about the old man's shoulders. For his supposed age, he had the architectural build of a strong warrior. Clothed all in dark garments, I could barely make out the definition of his physique. His snow-white, curly hair fed from his head all the way down to his beard. His long, bushy beard was an unsurprising stereotype of what one would consider, dare I say, a mage. His beard was at least fifty centimetres long and kept wonderfully in the shape of an upside-down, cultivated, snow-covered tree. A childish thought scurried cheekily into my head. Perhaps, if I were to live through this whole escapade, I could hide Jared's vegetables in there. At that point, he gave me a stern look through the sea-blue piercing wisdom of his eyes. Could he read my mind?

I tilted my head to the sand. So much was running though my head like a never-ending relay race. I did not even realise I was babbling everything out loud.

"Who… who are you? What do you want? Where is…?"

The man in the middle motioned a commanding hand forward that slapped an invisible cusp about my now tongue-tied mouth; even the tinkling of the rainfall seemed to hush.

"I am the Past," said the first.

"I, the Present," the second man continued.

The third man cleared his throat and swung on his heels for a brief moment before speaking.

"Yes, and I am Jeronaseph Holipthanusuki Talikupeothanio the sixth hundredth and eighty second."

I started blankly at him with eyebrows at high-noon attention.

His hand waved forward, as he scoffed cheekily, "That never works. Fine! I am the Future."

He cast a glare at the other two who looked back and smirked childishly; their supposedly manly entranced ruined by the one who should know best.

To me, none of this made sense. I still thought I was dead. Or subconscious? Unconscious! This could not be real! People did not just *appear* in real life.

The scream of what could only be perceived as a flying banshee screeched through the skies from the unknown distance. Above me – left, right, above – the boulders of noises were tumbling around me and the fingers of death were crawling towards my soul.

My nose began to run in the cold, obliterating my sense of smell. I had so many questions and so few answers that it seemed to clear any thought of care for my nose at that point. I just wanted to know if I was dead and where the heck that bright light was for me to follow.

"No child," the Future's voice metamorphosed into one authoritative, "you haven't died. You were right to come here. Not that it was by choice, but it was your destiny."

I tried to get my words out; to offer some resilience, but confusion riddled my mouth. I fumbled about in complete discombobulation, staring at them all in the unforgiving breath of frozen fury; somewhat embarrassed at my partial nakedness in front of them.

"You are one caught up in a shadow war, Malaki…"

"It's Mala…"

The Future waved his hands. His head diverted from me and towards the floor in disbelief that I had disrupted him. Even though he had pronounced my name incorrectly!

"Here have this."

Before my eyes could navigate towards the source of the paternal voice, I felt the firewood warmth of the Past's cloak crumple into my outspread arms. Although it looked so light and uselessly thin, as I put on the silky, soft satin, it filled me with the warmth of ten surrounding bonfires. In turn, I placed the hood of the cloak over my shivering head once I had pinned the cloak into place.

"Warm enough?" He smiled with reassuring eyes.

"Yeah… yeah thanks," I nodded in approval.

"You are caught up in a shadow war, child." The Future continued, "One in which you have no choice but to be a part of. One in which the forces of darkness have reared their ugly head against the world as we know it, and there is only one way to stop it. At the forefront of this shadow war is a formidable queen of sorrows which the history books will not compare to write about for fear of future generations being scarred with the memoirs of the past. One feasted upon by evil and darkness, greed and corruption, and tastes nothing but the coveting of subverting all that is good and pure known to us all. I have seen the death. I have seen the pain. I have seen the lack of courage in the hearts of men as they melt like snowmen in the ferocious forest fire. I have heard the children scream; the lost boy shouting for his mother. I have smelt the ash pour from the skies like confetti, blown in the wind of despair. I have tasted of the loss of all that are held dear to me in the two realms."

He paused and gazed at me.

"A shadow war which, indeed, was once held in the silence of the realms, but now the seal is broken, and the time to act has never been so necessary as it is now."

"Wha… what is it… he… she… what is…?"

"She goes by the name 'La Sombre Une'," the Future said.

My eyes dotted about the ground, as I blinked for memory to flag up what that meant.

"But that's French for…"

"Yes, child. La Sombre Une: 'Dark One'."

CHAPTER EIGHT
My Limit's the Sky

Lights hopscotched above the woman on the stretcher. The dotted halos passed by the eyes as they darkened from view, and a grunting filled the hallways.

The smell of bleach and antibacterial gel filled the nostrils of the carriers and the carried, as they zoomed towards the hub where God had brewed His new gift to two members of mankind.

The screeching and squealing of the wheels signalled a turn in this tooth-white tunnel.

"Nearly there, honey. Hold on!"

The grip of the contraction was like an unstoppable and inevitable wave of unseen force that flung a hammer on the target, and shot up the brick on the resounding gong.

"I'll take it from here, Doctor Stringer. Nurse Broom just beeped an emergency in Ward 21W for you to check out."

"But my… that's on the other side of…"

"I don't make the rules, Doctor. I've got this."

"Contractions are closer together now, Doctor Flynn," the miscellaneous voice of another midwife stated. "Every ten minutes now. The baby seems to be pretty active!"

The man stumbled with his words, as he watched helplessly; the queen of his heart being rushed off by the busy ants into the hub. The droplets of liquid frantically paced down his brow like a broken showerhead, and his wide, black eyes darted from white-coated person to person in search of some clarification or comfort or closure to the helpless situation.

He remembered his dear one's frequent words of religious utterance and pleas with the Heavenly Father for aid hoping that, at the very least, the Great God of his sweetheart would not bring her, or he whom she bore, any harm, or, at worst death. The thought of a final drumbeat of either heart would clash a cymbal of multiplied waves of sorrow into a world so lately filled with elation. The giggles of ear to tummy and grinning from ear to ear with both pride and excitement at the gurgling noises happening in the sanctuary; the silent moments of seeing his soulmate rest in the cloudy, covered tub; the mother ship floating in mahogany glory; glistening with a healthy glow like a chocolate fountain, as she hummed sweet nothings around the fingered circled upon her skin.

He recalled the moment his wife's eyes burst like a firework with ecstatic flare the first time the tiny soul kicked in the sanctuary; or was it a wobble of his tiny bottom; or his tiny hands curiously poking around his current abode where he would grow into the likeness of his mother and father, knitted fearfully and wonderfully by the one his wife would firmly declare 'the Lord Jesus'?

"Oh Jesus…" he whispered in flurried breath, "Lord Jesus, please help us."

The uncomfortable grunting of his wife echoed and resounded through the crashed doors that were flung to either side. They once stood gatekeepers of the maternity ward where soon, hopefully, the cause of all this grief would bring forth the effect of happiness and melted hearts, wrapped in a baby blanket and smothered in the warmth of his mother's bosom.

The unseen force began to tighten his grip on the sanctuary. This shot a pyramid of pain into the full construction in less than ten seconds, and lo, a clenched, closed hand from his dear wife was all the husband could perceive as a communication tool.

"Doctor... um... Doctor Flynn." He put his arm out in a flickering fashion; not wanting to hold the transporting units from reaching the delivery room which was only a few metres away now.

"Is the ba...? Is she...? Are they going to be okay?"

Doctor Flynn's face was barely visible. She had only appeared a few moments ago from the East Wing corridor; hands fastened with transparent gloves and hair fully covered with the paper mache helmet to, he supposed, get everyone through the crash course as cleanly as possible. Doctor Flynn looked like she was fresh out of university and into the fires of midwifery on the front-line trenches. This grenade was ready to blow, and Doctor Flynn looked cool, calm and collected. Her fresh face smiled gently at the exasperated father-to-be and told him that everything was going to be just fine.

"Most women who are very high risk are like thi..."

He zoned out in his own thoughts like an eager child in a tuck shop line. The question of how she even knew his name without any of the three other members of staff uttering or introducing him to her never had a chance to cross his mind in the busy queue of thoughts that skipped from one to the other.

The transporter had finally reached its destination, and the white-and-blue-dressed, trio of a crew worked to gather the frenzied atmosphere into a calm conclusion.

The CTG made its appearance.

"Okay, ma'am, I am just going to attach this belt around your abdomen."

"Wha… what does that do?"

"It is just a machine that monitors the baby's heartbeat. These two tennis ball-looking plates do just that." She smiled reassuringly at him while pointing the two eyes and ears towards the sanctuary. "One monitors the baby's heartbeat, and the other helps us see and know when each contraction happens and estimate how strong it will be."

"Hang in there, my love."

"Baby's heart rate is normal and steady."

The room was lit like the morning sunrise. Beams of light bounced off each reflection of the smooth, sandy pebble-coloured wall. The length and width were no more than a rectangular hub; ten by fifteen metres. The resuscitation machine confidently stood a few metres away in the corner of the room. The white-cased, quadruple-layered lifesaver was silent for now, and the expectant father hoped that it would remain that way. No need for any further crises today.

A large, rectangular window reflected the bodies in the delivery room. That was until Doctor Flynn hurriedly shut the outside spirits from prying in with queering, squashed faces on the solid, transparent barrier with her smooth, small hands.

"Okay ma'am. Today is the day your baby is going to be born."

Doctor Flynn spoke in words that soothed like the summer grass fields which matched her glistening, shamrock eyes.

"Is this your first?"

"Yes," she panted on the bed, "well, first birth at least. And by the pain that I am currently feeling it's going to be my…"

She winced and let in a deep breath through her tube-shaped mouth.

"…My last."

They did not really notice Dr Flynn pull out a syringe. She walked confidently, putting it in front of her face and flicking it on the clear cylinder that showed the translucent liquid. It bobbed from side to side and then stillness; joining in the game of hide-and-seek in silence, as Dr Flynn moved closer to the carrier and her other half.

"This should help with the pain."

Without waiting for a response, she grabbed the glowing, mahogany-brown arm of the carrier and twisted it around gently to find a vein on the thin-skinned underside of her right, dark elbow. The thin bee sting of the needle disappeared into the carrier.

She looked at her sweetheart with her soft, bark-brown hands upon her sanctuary. She looked into deep eyes of anxiety and, though she could feel a stream form down her left cheek and create a solid pool in the white layer between her and the mattress, she wanted him to know that in this sea of uncertainty, everything was going to be just fine. Though she was one with him, her heartbeat resounded in tune with the one in the sanctuary; she had known him for nearly a year longer than anyone else in the room had; than anyone else in the world. She had slept with him, eaten with him, drank with him, played with him, sang to him; and now she was finally going to introduce the unborn child to everyone else for the first time. Then her beloved, too, could hold him, read to him, grow with him; find joy with him.

She didn't mean what she said, although the nerves in the lower end of her back sent crashing signals to her brain, the constant envelope of signed, sealed and delivered agony to her midriff. She knew that all of the pain and suffering she was currently enduring would not compare to the rush of jubilation that would run through her veins when, with outstretched arms, she would embrace her firstborn son.

"Do please take a seat, sir," Doctor Flynn invited with outstretched palm to the somewhat pale purple chair placed next to his beloved by her pillow. He kissed her lovingly after gently brushing her long, spaghetti, soot-black hair to the back of her ear. His prickly, stubble prodded about her moist forehead.

"I love you," he whispered softly.

*** *** *** *** ***

He lifted her hand and put it into the middle of both of his. He felt the soft radiance of her lavender skin in between his anxiously humid hands. She squeezed his hand, as if to say thank you, but the firmer, unplanned grip let out a hint of desire for this particular burst of inner impetus to pass.

"I'll tell you a story, yeah?"

The words just fluttered out of his mouth. Out of them came wings of courage. The pitter-patter of his feet stopped with firm aplomb. His prayer had been answered. A wave of paternal peace had flown over him and the head of the household took his lead.

"In a town somewhere a little bit far from here," he began. "Well, I say a little…"

He chuckled and pointed his face to the bristling eggshell cream floor as he did.

"…Rather far from here, a young man in his late teens was at his family's market stall. The smell of the various fruit and vegetables on

each of the stacked shelves behind him;" He began to motion with his hand, "the apples, the bananas, the coriander, the mangos…"

"And who is this mysterious fruit and vegetable seller?"

He smiled a smile that showed a glacier-white beam of love and cheekiness into her soft gaze towards her lighthouse.

"He was obviously the most good-looking fruit and vegetable seller in all the land!"

He motioned his hands in a fashion to suggest that her question was loaded with rhetoric and rooted in cheeky sarcasm.

"Just picture him: sun-kissed, olive skin, tufty, curly, dark hair and endless dark, black eyes and white cauliflower ears."

She giggled sheepishly, remembering a fond memory of her own past.

"On this particular day, he was wearing his mossy green T-shirt which was worn under an obviously cool, navy blue and… rather stained, white cotton apron. His denim blue flared jeans were just as stylish back then too, by the way, I should add."

He pointed at her, poking her knee, which was resting on top of her other leg, as he did so. She, on the other hand, was unable to stop her giggle turn into a chime of laughter that warmly filled the atmosphere.

"Hey! I will have you know that baggy, flared jeans were cool back then!"

"You mean tents?"

"They were good for… er… the breeze… You know… it was nice for the, er… legs…"

The chime of laugher turned into a small orchestra between them that rang the bells in their hearts in unison.

"Ooh… oh!"

She touched the top of the sanctuary with one hand; fingers spread out like a stethoscope on the beating chest of a patient; trying to control the rate of her laughter and breathing as she did so.

"Are you okay, my love?"

The worried voice reared his head.

She opened her eyes and nodded tiredly.

"Carry on, darling."

"His red and black-laced, blue trainers splashed quietly across his little kingdom, as he shouted out the latest deals."

He got up and imitated a man in a marketplace enticing customers to his stall.

"Come on, madam! A deal for you today, sir, on the finest peppers and green beans in town. I'm here all day, but the fruit is not allowed to stay!"

"Ha ha – Sit down, silly."

He flopped back into the chair with youthful vitality and ran his fingers backwards through his forest of dark hair. He gently placed her hand back into his and played invisible hopscotch with his fingers in her resting, open palm.

"So, the streets were filled and busy as usual. The marketplace was buzzing with people like honeybees going from stalk to stalk and gathering whatever pollen they needed to take out to their own nests. The young man had made a few good sales during the day. The dark, cloudy sky had recently changed its tune, and the song that now sung was a golden reflection of the firmament on the earth.

He paused.

"There was, in the midst of all this buzz, this one honeybee…"

He bit his bottom lip and looked into her eyes. A moment of communication took place that no one else in the room could interpret.

"Oooh… I'll do the next bit." She reshuffled slightly on the couch.

"Okay. Go."

He gently guided a floating few strands of hair away from her face with his warm hands.

"Well… this honeybee had flown all the way from a land that was much farther away from this land, and indeed where the mysterious

fruit and vegetable seller was from. On this particular day, she and her high school classmates, some of the most recent school-leavers, had decided not to go into one of the nearby cities but to check out the local scenery and its… produce. She had just had a bit of a fall out with one of her girlfriends the same morning, and so she was a bit upset with the whole affair."

"What happened?"

She flicked him on the point of his nose with her finger. Her diamond stone, silver engagement ring sat elegantly over her matching, silver-plated wedding ring.

"Shh. Never you mind about that. Anyway, that day, she had her silky smooth, black hair tied up in one of the multicoloured, brown bows her mother had given her as a birthday present the year before. They had eventually ended up in the marketplace a few hours later.

"Gosh. The place was alive with noise and people. She had this beautiful, golden-brown dress and cute, little shoes, and yes, she was presently shouting silent curses at the skies for nearly ruining her sensitive hair. The last thing she needed was to be walking around advertising the next wonder of the world: a morphing thicket on a human head!"

She imitated a growing frock of hair; eyes widening. He, on the other hand, chuckled babyishly at her antics.

"Yeah, I've seen that thicket before," he said cheekily, cuddling himself like a naughty boy in a schoolyard and smirking lovingly.

She opened her mouth in sarcastic shock and threw a red and golden-laced cushion at him.

"Excuse me! You said it didn't look that bad!"

She gasped again and turned about her to find another weapon, but he had already piped up, giggling, with arms stretched out in submission.

"Okay! I'm joking. I'm joking!"

"Uh-huh…"

She jerked her neck in a circle and satirically looked away, facing briefly at the low-lit lamp that hung above the red and blue-flowered vase in the corner of the room.

He dropped carelessly on the couch and grabbed her hand which was currently signalling him to "stop there" rather than give her the high five he triumphantly slapped.

"Go on, darling."

He cupped his fingers in hers.

"Nope."

"Please. Please? Pleeaaasssseeeee?"

"Alright. Alright!"

She turned in giddy excitement. Not too quickly though; it was not just them in the room.

"So, fortunately, this girl was clever, as she carried her emergency, black umbrella in her handbag wherever she went. She was rather peckish and something fresh was just what she wanted. She heard the multiple voices of both men and women competing for her mind's attention. The heavens had just finished displaying its finest display of watercolour, and the soothing sun had begun its patchwork of golden grandeur in the pockets of the ground.

"In trying to pack her umbrella in its white and black polka-dot sleeve, she dropped her phone to the floor. She couldn't turn quickly enough to save it before the inevitable crack and splatter of technology; the cry of which would not be heard under the noise above us all. But a hand, swift as the day follows the night, managed to catch it before it crashed and splashed on to the ground."

The glow of the room's fire cast their shadows on to the blonde-coloured wall behind them.

"And then she saw him…"

"And then he saw her."

"And she saw him turn and fire through the crowds with her

phone. He didn't stop for want of logic or morality, but only greed and robbery."

"Hey, that's not fair. He was…"

"…A crook; a crook who took advantage of an obviously foreign victim on home ground. She didn't really know what to do. To scream or shout in such a crowded place was not really her style. But, boy, please; this was her phone! She shouted, 'Hey! He has my phone! Someone help!' "

"And then her saw her," he said softly.

"And she saw him."

"And he saw him; dashing through the bustling crowd, a few metres ahead, and running in his direction. He picked up a few of his finest and hardest potatoes from his stall and aimed and fired!"

He dramatised the whole scene like a superhero on the couch.

"Pah. He threw the first one… which hit an old woman, who was fiercely telling her granddaughter off, on the side of her head!"

They howled in laughter. She wiped a joyful tear from her eye.

"He threw two more. One hit him in the crook of the shoulder and he was clearly unnerved. The hero then threw another…"

"Which eventually hit the puddle on the ground, where the poor victim was then pacing, and the splash from the murky water sprayed all over her dress and shoes!"

"Ha ha, yes."

"And she is stood there thinking, What the actual foolishness?!"

"But then he clearly saw that the potatoes had failed and darted towards the hooded hound."

"She now had had her phone stolen and a freckle-faced dress."

"He tackled the thief into some other fishmonger's stall and managed to unhand the phone from the man."

He shrugged his shoulders and gave himself a swipe of the shoulder, with masculine confidence, as he did so with raised eyebrows.

"And then he saw her."

"And she smelt him."

She tucked her lips in and giggled; her shoulders jerking up and down like a piledriver.

"Hey! I smelt good!" He sniffed. "For a waterless aquarium."

She burst out with hearty laughter that warmed the fire in her heart.

"Ha ha, let me get a tissue."

She began to get up from the couch, steadily.

"Oh no," he insisted cautiously, "I'll go."

"No, no." She placed one hand on her back and the other on his lap. "It's okay; I could do with some movement anyway."

She pushed herself up slowly from the three-metre long, cream couch. She picked up the tall glass of water and shuffled like a penguin around the corner archway and out of sight into the kitchen.

"Do you want anything?" the familiar voice came to his ears.

"No, thank you."

He sat with hairy hands behind his head and stared at the simmering fireplace.

"Hey, love. I don't think I ever told you the name of the hero in this story…"

"Oh yeah, what is his name?"

"His name is…"

Crash.

A shatter.

Like a bullet fired through a glasshouse of Jenga.

It came from the other room.

*** *** *** *** ***

"Doc… Doctor Fly… I can't see the room. I can… I can't see!"

The wires and tubes were spiralled all over the wall behind the bed. Monitors and multiple little screens were flickering and blinking, but he was only able to focus on the apple of his eye.

"What do you mean? Is it…?"

"The whole room is blurred. It is as if… I don't know… what is going…?"

"Just try not to panic, love; the b…"

Dr Flynn calmly walked to the bed from the middle of the delivery room, looked at a random monitor's screen and hummed to herself. She now had a white surgical mask on; the tooth-white doctor's coat was now buttoned from neck to shin.

"There is nothing to panic about, madam. It is just because of the…"

"I… I can't… I can't hear you any more. It is all mumbled noise!"

"Doctor, what is going on?"

"Sir, I am going to have to ask you to leave briefly."

"I am not…"

She lay on the bed somewhat helpless. To move placed her in intricate pain regardless of whatever limb sought to voice their opinion. She could feel the push from the sanctuary grow stronger, and the culmination of all things was about to close its curtains for the final showdown. She was completely, currently unreconciled with her senses and was trying not to panic for the sake of the coming explorer. She tried to make out her husband and the doctor.

Were they by the door?

A figure left the room.

Or at least that was what it looked like.

"Doctor? Doctor. The baby…"

The unforeseen force clasped again. In the next few moments, whether she realised it or not, the sanctuary was delivering the fruit of its nine-month labour.

Her beloved was now outside the delivery room. He tugged his cotton-black hair with both hairy hands and tried his hardest to hold in every ounce of fear and anxiety that was boiling inside of him. The corridor was not exactly brimming with people; in fact, it was rather quiet. The parallel, linear lights above him and across the hall were the only companions of hope that he had at that moment.

Far across the twenty-yard, rice-white corridor, the only sounds emanating were those distant cries from the other few delivery rooms in the hall.

Would one come from where he had left?

A wail from a baby emanated a break in between a multitude of voices in the man's head. He darted his head at the door, eyes zoning to the middle of it to see the slightest change of light that would take place at the slightest swing of the door.

No.

Not his own.

His black-and-white-striped top was creased with the many motions of madness that the day had borne down on him. As he now sat on the plastic-cushioned, metal chair directly in front of the room where his beloved was, he saw many dancing shadows passing the door in somewhat of a manic frenzy.

Was what she'd said to him, before he left the room, really the case?

A flash of light escaped under the crevice of the two-inch-thick door. He twitched his eyebrows in curiosity.

What was that?

Probably just one of the lights from one of the many machines in the room he supposed. He got up from the lonesome chair and began to walk up and down the corridor. For him, the past few moments had taken the meaning of time to a completely new dimension. If you'd asked him how long he was there for; how long he'd spent trying to steady his thumping heartbeat; how long he'd spent reminding himself of all the promises he'd made to himself – how he was going to be a good dad. No; a great dad. Not like his own father, who'd left when he was six. He certainly would not be able to tell you the number of times his hairy hands had pressed into his thick thighs which were covered by his navy blue, denim jeans; or the amount of times he'd got up and sat down like a meerkat peering over the marshlands.

As he walked towards the double doors that separated the two corridors, he failed to notice the halogen bright, blue and white glimmer of light that flooded under the delivery room door behind him for the next three steps he took.

He turned around to continue the stride and stretch of his legs to the other end of the corridor. Looking at the signs and other print on the wall was a nice distraction for him. As he travelled down the stone, grey-floored corridor, he saw a shadow overtaken by a straight angle of light.

"Sir?"

A female voice appeared.

"Are you ready?"

*** *** *** *** ***

"Yes."

He rubbed his fingers together and eventually spread his hands out across the cool collection of black-and-white notes; the crescendo of his heartbeat thumping through his fingers, as he placed them over A minor.

A brief silence filled the air until his left hand calmly opened the hum of music into the ether. The music interlude of A minor to G, and G to C, and furthermore to G filled the room in soft sound.

*** *** *** *** ***

"Can you hear that?"

Was she talking to him? He recognised the short distance between the two of them and realised that she'd appeared from the delivery room his beloved was in.

A woman walked calmly out of the door; looking somewhat cautiously towards the corridor away from him to begin with. Her sea-blue shirt and white trousers certified to him that she was one of the midwives who were with his beloved.

*** *** *** *** ***

I'm tired of hearing the same old song
Paint the same picture with a different face
I never thought life could turn out to be with this way.

As unpredictable as life is
I try to come to terms with the thought of losing you
Because I know that the next time I see you could be my last.

*** *** *** *** ***

His eyes began to flood, and his humid hands covered his nose and mouth in quiet hope and prayer.

"Is... is she okay?"

QUANTUM

*** *** *** *** ***

I guess I always over thought my words
Overstated my own expressions
I never thought the meanings of those words could take effect.

As the tears begin to scatter
The blindness doesn't matter; the touch is good enough
I never thought the outcomes of your actions could turn this way.

*** *** *** *** ***

The woman stood at an angle towards him; one foot held open the door. Her distinctively crystal-blue eyes met his reddening windows to his soul.

"Yes." She smiled warmly at him. "Yes, she is."

Her blossoming rosy cheeks beamed warmth and certainty in his direction. She stood confidently at five foot eight inches; her timber-brown, long, straight hair was consciously swept behind her head and laid over her left shoulder.

He tried to move quicker towards her, but all of a sudden, he hit an invisible brick wall of anxiety, and it juddered him backwards, as the lead balloon fell on his heart of courage. The corridor around him bridged further and further away with every quickening breath his lungs exhaled; inhaled; exhaled.

*** *** *** *** ***

Soon you'll be lost
And so will my chance
Need to pick up the pieces
There were at first glance
The birds may sing, and soar up high
Somehow I know my limit's the sky.

*** *** *** *** ***

"I… I ca… I can't do it."

She paused for a moment. She looked warmly at him. The door closed stealthily behind her, as she took a few steps towards him and placed a hand on his shuddering shoulder.

"You are going to make a great father and a doting husband. The family that you have been blessed with is, without a doubt, one that is gifted from God. You…"

"You don't understand!" He purposed to turn away from her so she didn't see a tear roll down his shivering cheek. "He left me! What if I…"

*** *** *** *** ***

I'm tired of feeling the same emotions
Write the same figure with a different pen
I never thought life could turn out to be this way.

*** *** *** *** ***

"Leave them?" she replied. "That is out of the question. Your heart is not the heart of your father's…"

*** *** *** *** ***

And as I grow older,
Never mind the wiser, I'm brought to different scenes
Though some things are better left to be unturned.

I guess I always believed in my dreams
My safety net where I could be free
I never thought life would make me feel uneasy
And as the strains begin to tighten
I find it hard to share a close reunion
I never expected life to turn out to be this way.

*** *** *** *** ***

"…whilst we may all be from the line of Adam, and indeed are crushed under the same fall, we do not all follow the same path of destiny."

*** *** *** *** ***

"Did you really write that yourself?" The humbled question resonated a few metres away from the one who had played the memoirs of his childhood in the open air.

"Yes I did," he said whilst comforting himself by rubbing his forearm with his other hand. "It was all about and for him."

"I think it is really beautiful."

*** *** *** *** ***

The broken dam within his eyes was sealed with the comforting words that had rested upon his ears and spirit.

"That person is not the man that you are. We live in realms of broken promises and sometimes cracked dreams, but you have to realise that there are two people in that room who need you to go in now and be there for them; to comfort them; to love them; because you have no idea the effect that all that you do is going to have on them, and…"

She paused slightly and looked at the ground momentarily.

"…and even the world. Don't lose sight of that."

"You are right."

He looked at her with reassured eyes. His whole adult life had come to the end of a chapter, and another was about to begin.

"Come on then, sir. Let's introduce you to someone special."

As the double doors gently opened, a willing and new man entered in. He saw the very familiar room as he'd left it, but with one more person visibly occupying it.

Where was Dr Flynn?

He walked over to his beloved who beamed radiantly at him. She held the apple of their eyes on her bosom; the little creation wrapped in a fluffy and warm, butterfly-blue blanket.

She caressed the baby gently; her bed propped up at a 45-degree angle, as she now sat comfortably on the soft, white sheet on the bed.

"It's a boy," his beloved said, as she raised her arms to him to pass him his heir. "You win the bet." She smiled warmly at him.

He pouted his mouth at the baby, as a tear jogged down his cheek. All the anticipation, the anxiety, the worry, it all got washed away as the baby, freshly wrinkled and plump, smiled at him with those dark, bark-brown eyes. His dark black hair was wetly strewn from side to side over his head, and his little, tiny fingers danced carefully at his nose, taking in the oxygen in the air, and feeling the heartbeat of his father pulse through his hands for the very first time.

"How are you? Your eyes? Your ears?"

"I'm all well," she said tiredly, "thank you, love. I think I just need some rest now."

Unknown shoeprints on the ground lay unrecognised.

"I will leave you three to have some time alone."

The woman who had only recently counselled the new father humbly began to make her way to the door.

"Thank you for everything," she said. "Thank you very much. To you and to…"

"You are more than welcome. Every life is indeed precious."

As she opened the door, the new father hop-stepped carefully towards her and cleared his throat; hoping to grab her attention.

"Er… Thank you… for earlier…"

She smiled kindly again at him. "The pleasure is all mine."

As she left, she turned around once more.

"Have you… thought of a name for your son?"

He looked proudly at his son, and then to his wife, and lastly to the author of the question.

"Yes, we have."

He smiled at his son.

"We shall call him…"

CHAPTER NINE
Inception

"What kind of name is that?"

"There is not much time to explain, Malachi."

The Present stood still in the solid moment of time. The here and now was where we were at. His words commanded a stillness in my heart that rendered my stubbornness frozen.

No.

I had questions, and those questions needed answering.

The tick-tock tapping of the falling rain splattered into drip drops of dark soil and mud. Casper (the fog) was staring at us from every circular angle in the thick blanket of the dark night. The backstage crew were silently closing every door of escape, and I was taking part in the final curtain call.

A claw of lightning tore through the sky, lashing a whip of conscious reality to the situation. The electric line across the horizon had brought streaks of barbed wire across the furious firmament. The photographer in the sky's camera gave the momentary opportunity to see a distinct nimbus cloud stampeding towards us from the horizon.

What was that?

The electric jolt jump-started a quickening pulse throughout my body. As I looked up at the heavens, I could make out the anguished faces of the grey and black skulls that twisted and contorted in the billowing winds. The glow of the sun was completely eradicated and so was the enlightening reality of the light that I once knew.

The man who had recently told me he was the Past instinctively crossed his right hand over to his left hip where his weapon lay. His head angled at the heavens slightly, his bicep tensed as his wrist twisted in anticipation. The golden-laced, cherry-red scabbard was instantly attractive as it intertwined like golden ivy along the scarlet undertone. Waiting to execute his master's command.

Waiting to execute anyone who might be trying to save me perhaps?

Could I trust these people?

Could I trust my mind?

What if these people were not who they said they were?

What if they were the enemy?

The warmth of the cloak that I wore invited a kinetic rush over the thousands of goosebumps that were now melting from the surface of my skin. As I breathed in the chilled air around me like a panting dog that is excited to see its master return home (minus every ounce of excitement), I could feel the icy vapour work its way into my lungs; the little, red blood cell workers carrying the thawing oxygen icicles around the channels of my body.

Sludgy sand built its fortress around my toes which itched at the invading army of granules from every side. The soles of my feet fluttered through waves of warmth and tricks of cold air, as the robe swayed from side to side.

"You have to come with us, Malachi."

The Present looked at me with his freshly cut grass eyes. He took a step towards me and, as he did, the sole of his staff rode out of the ground to reveal another glowing tip.

He was visibly able to grip his strong hands around the bold staff with ease. He opened his left hand toward me in friendly gesture. A few strands from the fringe of his straw-yellow hair fell across his brow as he did so.

"Take my hand, Malachi. We shall explain everything when we are somewhere safe."

I took a step back, my eyes widening in synced multiplication of questions that I had swirling in my head.

Was this really it?

Or perhaps, the question I should be asking was, 'What really was it?'

"No." I shook my head sheepishly. "I am not going anywhere. Where is my mum? My brother? Where is my da…?"

"Malaki…"

"It's Malachi!"

The drumbeat in my chest echoed, as I clung the robe, with both hands, around my body.

The Future moved towards me carefully. As he took a step forward, he lowered the Present's arm with his hand. His robe slithered in the sand with each step he took in my direction. Each breath of mine seemed somewhat shorter than the previous one.

Was he going to kill me? Had he had enough? Their prey was not listening, and this was not the place for him to be shouting back in defiance.

"My dear boy, time is of the essence."

Lightning tore through the sky and cackled down at us.

"This shadow war is about to pierce itself into the light, and we only have a short opportunity before the wheels of time themselves are written." He paused and looked into the windows to my soul. "We cannot take that chance."

The Past was half turned towards the darkness. His feet were placed at an angle, as if at any moment he would, if he could, propel himself like a javelin into the air and strike at the heart of the aerial carrier of sorrow. His heel was flicked up slightly in the sludge of sand like a gladiator against the mob, against the crowd, peering from left to right like a cautious crow at the faceless faces in the distance.

"You, Malaki, are special; even though you do not know it yet. Destiny does not give you the choice to choose. It chooses you."

I had a mixture of a soothed ego and a terrifying cauldron of confusion swirl in every nook and cranny of my conscience. Whatever the reason, I could tell that these three men were either very serious (and it was perhaps a very good idea if I joined them wherever they planned to go), or very crazy (and someone needed to carry them away). On the other hand, was what they were saying any less ridiculous than the meteorological tirade that was encircling us like a tornado of frothing hyenas?

"Why is this La Sombre Une…? Why is she doing this? How did she…?"

"She was once… like us," the Future began. "Something happened…"

He paused and cast his head down in deep thought; angling his chin to the ground. As he turned, I could just about make out the last fingers of ink that spread its tendrils about his clavicle. I couldn't see much, but before I'd had a chance to stare for any useful length of time, the Future turned back to me.

"La Sombre Une is born of hate and darkness, a spirit of relentless wrath and with a cunning desire to see the end of all that is hopeful and charitable in us all. The Book of…"

"Jero."

The Present cut the cord of the conversation.

"Take it slowly with the guy. It is all a bit too much for him already at the moment."

His voice was finally tuned with command and respect. I was a little frustrated that he had cut off my only piece of knowledge at present (no pun intended). I hadn't noticed how wide my eyes had become; acting like a sponge with every word that the Future had just spoken.

I blinked as if someone had just blown forcefully into my eyes. I hadn't noticed the lack of feeling in the tips of my fingers; the robe had been clung about me so tightly that I'd forgotten about the need for blood to flow through to them.

"We are running out of time."

The Past's head did not turn around in politeness to make eye contact with us, but his voice managed to find its way to his audience, planting within me a sense of fear, urgency and anticipation.

Time for what?

Why was he looking as if he was preparing to attack the very number of stars in the galaxy?

His bicep began to contract, and his elbow rose ever so slightly. The silent shiver of his tar-black sword appeared; the golden ivy twined across the foot of the weapon.

I gazed with mouth ajar at the sight of the soldier. All of a sudden, he darted like a possessed gazelle into Casper.

My vocal cords tingled; the strings of the harp vibrating under the gentle strike of the index finger. I opened my mouth to utter a shout, a scream, to tell him it was too dangerous. My hand stretched out like a lost child in a crowded town plaza at the distancing guardian.

"He'll be fine."

The Future raised his hand, in what seemed like supersonic speed, and gently rested his warm-blooded finger upon my quivering lips. His arm slotted through the slit in the side of his silky, whale-blue cloak and revealed an intricate alignment of tattoos that ran from the back of his strong hand, and continued the marathon, into his cloak.

As I looked cross-eyed at his finger, my eyes journeyed along the pastel, cream-skinned arm of patchwork. It looked as if someone had taken the inner parts of a watch and laced the whole workings out in barbed wire; tying them around his slightly wrinkled skin. The circular balance conjoined along the intertwining barbed wire to the pillar plate – the big hand directing the viewer to the spring, the centre wheel – Roman numerals running in sporadic fashion about his muscular arm.

My eyes climbed up his shoulders; they ascended up through his clustered cloud of a wise, chalky beard and into his paternal-looking eyes.

Could I trust him? Them? Whatever he was doing, he was trying to tell me silently with that look in his mature face that I could trust him. Whatever he was doing, he was saving face very well.

Out of them all, whilst he was frustratingly unable to say my name, he was the one who, in my view, had made most effort to make me feel comfortable. If I was in his shoes, I would hopefully try and be as patient with me as possible, if indeed, he was telling the truth and I did need to listen to them instead of wasting time asking questions.

The Future slowly lowered the silencer from my mouth.

A great drum roll of thunder crashed from the heavens on to the victim earth again. The shackles of the unseen beast rumbled and ricocheted on to the ground where we were. The Future took a step back from me to survey the metallic symphony above.

I had not even realised that the Present had disappeared too. And then I remembered that there was one question that had yet to be answered.

"My family... Jared? My mum?"

The Future's eyes had not moved from his aerial survey.

"I asked you a que..."

"They will be fine."

Fine?

Fine? Fine was not good enough! Had he not just stated that the whole earth had now been plunged into doom? A piece of my heart broke as I thought about my family; my mum, Dad, Jared, suffering at the hands of whatever evil was out there.

Why me?

Why now?

For what purpose?

"Bu... but you said everywhere has been plunged into darkness!"

*** *** *** *** ***

The roar of the cloudy lion had flung his authority again in the dark, dreary scene I so often remembered; I so often lay awake at night wide-eyed in the cloak of dripping sweat.

Jero was right to be cautious.

To be honest, so much had changed since I'd come out of the watery prison from the time only moments ago I was a somewhat naive teenage boy. Only so recently I had been surrounded by the loving hedge of my family, scoffed at the scolding of my caring mother and batted back the advice of my doting dad.

He was right. As I stood there contemplating the whole matter, the whole concept of life not being as clear-cut as I had once imagined; good, evil...

The world had indeed been plunged into darkness, but not the whole earth was in the sort of darkness that I thought he was talking about, or perhaps you are thinking about.

You see, a shadow is not necessarily absent just because you cannot see it. A shadow only chooses to reveal itself depending on what angle of light you cast at it. Shadows are everywhere; a very loud part of creation that the world is all too silent about. The shadow war queen had sought to finish the game of chess with no prisoners, only death; a checkmate was the final move she was willing to make.

*** *** *** *** ***

"Chess, child, is a game of strategy and patience."

His arm had now disappeared back into his cloak along with the silencer. Glimpses of the tick-tock biology of tattoos flickering through the fabric in the quickening breeze from time to time.

"They have been taken care of."

"What does that f...?"

"Watch out!"

Before the words registered as a warning siren within my ears, I felt like I had zoned out into an out-of-body experience; as if my viewpoint had changed to a revolving camera on the inner circle of Casper's eight to ten-metre circumference.

The cloudy mist danced at its entrance in front of me and, from its cloudy portal, first a hand stretched and thrust forward, towards us, followed by the desperate face of the Past. Freckles of mud had splashed themselves on to his

117

wet face. Teams of watery canoes had trekked all over his skin-hugging, white T-shirt. His eyes fastened on to me in a state of morbid fear and determination; his hair strands bouncing in motion with the heavy footsteps that soon appeared in the twisting outer fog.

As the camera zoomed around and behind me, the Present was seen coming from a few metres to the right of the Past. He was already mid gallop through the air; the impala that leaped confidently across the chasm between the barren land and the field of harvest. The golden eye on his staff pinpointed the angle of it which was in perfect parallel to his mid-air frame. The aqua sky dwellers had also dramatically played into the fabric of his robe, which was presently risen in slow motion like a magic carpet behind him; his silver-surfaced, clock-faced pin grabbing the cloak together by his neck. Each tear from the maleficent sky was soaking its wet river into the thread of his baggy attire.

An arrow sliced through the ceiling of the inner circle.

It cut though time and space so quickly that I didn't realise…

The gust of wind shot past my eyes and, somehow, I began to feel gravity lose his natural command on my piece of earth. A brief, yet timeless weightlessness was felt, as I rose helplessly into the air; as if picked up and tossed by a master baker kneading bread. My arms, without any autonomous conviction or authority, flung out in front of me; in some way, shape or form hoping to attempt to formulate a plan to save or break my impending fall.

The camera swooped around the inner circle.

The cloak I had been given now fumbled in the air like a tossed napkin above an air vent.

I could not remember whether I hit the floor with my head or face first, but whatever happened next was a bit of a blur.

I could taste the bitter dregs of the earth about my palate and teeth. The grit and stone had tied companionship with the frothing saliva that was beginning to foam in my mouth. A shooting pain erupted in the centre of my face; the blood vessels in my nose bursting profusely at the loud knocking at its door. My vision was flicking through channels of black and haze; the sort of vision you get when you stand up too quickly and the blackout inside your mind presents itself before you as a stumbling block. The goosebumps began to grow and mountainously erupted about my body, and I felt the sensual tickling of sand and water squelching under the weight of my unwillingly mangled abdomen and legs.

"Grab his other arm!"

"I told you we…"

"…short window…"

"No now!"

"…shouldn't have spent so long!"

"…Laden…"

"Did you tell him that we were there when…?"

Helping hands ushered me to my limping feet, and my failing eyes murmured for vision in hopscotch fashion. In patches of vision, I lifted my head and noticed the Future fumbling for something on his person.

My body felt the warmth of ten fireplaces in one, as the robe no doubt clothed my shivering body for the second time. My toes nervously clenched the stiffening sand beneath, as I fumbled like a fawn trying to regain composure of my stance.

I gathered strength to look up into the sky, as the photographer grabbed my attention. Was that…?

He looked like…

He looked like…

I blinked and squinted like an old man, who'd forgotten his glasses, at home trying to read the terms and conditions of his final will; as if his very inheritance hung on to this last chance he had. Perhaps this was going to be the finale of my unconsciousness.

Only older…

Perhaps I was indeed going to wake up on that sun-kissed land after a nightmare of an underwater experience; spluttering with red-soaked eyes around the many hairy, or young, or small, or feminine legs supporting worried and relieved faces as I tried to pronounce to the crowd that I was okay.

Not so much older.

I blinked for hope of better vision, but the only aid that I found was the juddering focal point of my eyes.

Five or Six years?

"Have you got…?"

"If we don't do this now, all is…"

"He is bleeding ba…"

Don't be ridiculous, Malachi. Why on earth would you be floating in the air like an angel?

I know him…

Unless I was already dead?

*** *** *** *** ***

I could sense the anxiety, the confusion, the pain; but telling him now would only be futile. It would only make this harder than it already was.

*** *** *** *** ***

"Got it!"

The Future pulled out what looked like a pouch from underneath his cloak and solidly purposed his feet in our direction.

"Who... who is...?"

Before I could collect my thoughts, he turned away to face the darkening smog with a sense of severe satisfaction on his face.

Who was that man in the sky? The repeated flashbacks of blurry vision offered a momentary glimpse at the author of the flying arrow of death.

I, on the other hand, was not impressed (not that I had the capacity to do anything about it anyway). Had this been the prey from above that had just tried to kill me?

The arrow was one of the darkest-looking sources of death that I could make out.

Probably because this one was personal.

It was as if the black of the night harboured its children of hate and malice into the churning shape of the wicked arrow.

"You'll be fine, Mal..."

"...ust hang on!"

But the killer... that guy...

He looked just like me!

Perhaps I was dying.

Perhaps this was it; the end of my life.

Some say that there is an element of awareness when one crosses the valley from life into death. Perhaps this one was for me.

"Who was? He? Was tha... me?"

"We have no such time!"

I could feel consciousness slipping away from me. I became that little bit more aware that my breathing was slowed down. Words were unable to form in my mouth; the whole affair was a babbling mess. The weight of my lungs lay under a sack of potatoes and the pumping of my heart thumped for recess. The curtains above my eyes were being raked down by the deteriorating surplus of energy that my body had tried to hold on to.

Casper began to close in the ranks.

The splatter of the heavenly hose poured down sprinkles of heavy hail and icy water upon us.

Before the veil shut, I felt the solid fastening of three pairs of hands, like seat belts on a rollercoaster ride, secure me.

Sparkles of what looked like fairy, firefly dust floated around me.

Us.

Was this it? Was I going to Heaven?

If so, at least it had been verified that I was not delusional; that I did die. For the second time within those few minutes, I sensed a weightlessness overcome me; as if I were a bubble blown from a ring.

The light tried to seep into the crevices of my eyelids, but after the next struggle for breath, the fight was over. The battle for my life had been lost. The journey ends for some sooner than others. No need to press the timer on this game of chess. My pawns, my knights, my rook; all had left me. My father, my mother, my brother; no compass could find them to bring us together for one last time to share a moment. No need to gather the strategy board. I was the chessboard lampoon king facing death by fiery arrows.

Checkmate.

CHAPTER TEN
A Ripple in Time

Light filled the afternoon sky like an explosion of dandelion fairy dust. The rays of sublime sunlight bounced from cotton cloud to cotton cloud and descended on to the land below like fireflies in a frenzied ovation of joy and celebration. You could just about make out the array of winged creatures dotted in the sky.

A small flock of swallows danced in the smooth breeze and swooped down to the earth below with grace and poise, while the dandelion seeds made a quick yet elegant escape from the string, stalk prison below and floated effortlessly on the waves of the wind. And as they swung by the nest of the fire-breasted robin, who perched over her chocolate-freckled, blue eggs, she chirruped a sweet hymn. She chirped a melody that communed in harmony with the other robins in the shrub which appeared to be a green mesh seized by brown barbs holding the leaves together in a world inhabited by hopscotching robins and insects that interlocked in flight with each other as they tap-danced from branch to branch.

The dew of the vast land smelled so fresh, it was as if you were infused with a natural fragrance which the glistening, green grass permeated as it played; bending its body in a repetitive fashion against the cool, swift wind. Within the maze of green pasture was an array of flowers that whispered sweet nothings to the lustful bumblebees who had hauled their large bodies from petal to petal; completely intoxicated by the loving glucose of the flowers' pollen lips. The black-and-yellow-clothed staff tirelessly hovered from blue to yellow, and red to pink, not knowing the parody that, at the end of their shift, they would return to their queen as a rainbow-coloured harlequin.

If you were quick enough, you would have noticed the red-and-black-clothed lady sprint into flight in the air like a rubber band shot by the class clown into the atmosphere.

The light buzzing from her fluttering wings was silenced by the great cry of the snow-white-headed eagle in the sky above her. His brown feathers cascaded around his neck, as he sailed in the wind. His wings were his sail; spread out, spanning four feet from left to right. His strong stature was his mast. His curved maize-yellow beak, acting as the captain's call for his battle cry, was his bowsprit, and his duvet-white-feathered tail was his stern. As he anchored himself, like a buoy in the ocean-blue sky, his night-black pupils, surrounded by his mustard-yellow iris, focused on its goal.

He flapped his wings with an effortless swat and surged through the sky like a battleship towards its target.

Silver-blue fireflies, rising like smoke in the cool air, had his attention. The white, rising ashes were coming from the centre alleyway of this grand building's grounds. He anchored down the aerial highway; his telescopic eyes not wavering from his destination. His peripheral vision gave sight to the broccoli-topped trees, in the grand forest of the vast landscape, as he soared majestically over the multiple green-coloured rooftops.

Above a circular, one-mile patch of carefully cut grass he glided. Tens upon tens of dotted, clusters of people, who now gave up their undivided attention, flocked like moths to a flame to the source of the now fading, rising dots of light; the same smoke signal was planted around the east wing of the building.

The battlement had its heel rooted firmly in the lush, green ground, as it stretched its long, rectangular back in linear fashion for one hundred straight yards. The sturdy formation of brick-red, hewn stone created the armour of this fortress; dotted with horizontal windows that illustrated the three levels on the inside of the building. Solid, linear formations of light burst through the clear glass of each window, and the eagle's swift shadow slashed past each one.

The weight shifted from one side to the other, as he flurried past the north side of the sturdy castle. He slid through the twenty-metre gap, in between the north-west, side turret, where some of the rooms were located. Glades of forest encompassed the site behind the sleeping blocks, the rushing colours of mahogany wood glittering past the eagle's attention, as he narrowed the distance between him and the landing site; the cobbled streets of the Guild racing behind him like a plane above a runway. Zooming shades of stone-grey marble flashed past his vision like a fast-forwarded cassette tape.

The different coloured heads, bobbing up and down, began to get bigger and bigger, as he descended. The many startled and puzzled faces veered into focus, as he lowered to the ground. The particle cannon of light was now diminishing, and the transporters began to materialise into focus. He cawed out into the crowd to warn of his impending touchdown, the warning bell resounding in the ears of the many heads that turned to look above.

The eagle arched back like a racing dog forcefully restrained on a lead, as he overtook the blonde-haired man slightly below him and, in a matter of seconds, the eagle morphed into a man closing towards the ground. He landed and strode in perfect harmony through the growing murmur of people. Black, suede shoes now formed part of the gathering gallop of buffaloes to the flare. Tea-stain-coloured combat trousers were fastened by his leather, black belt around his waist. A noticeable, brass eagle head centred his abdomen as the buckle of his belt. It flickered in the passing shots of luminosity from the overhanging ball of light in the midst of the crowd. Similarly tea-brown, fingerless gloves cloaked around his clenched fists, and a night-black, cotton T-shirt rose and fell with each inhalation and exhalation of breath. He walked assuredly with a slightly open mouth; his jet-black eyes focused on the subject before him. His Chinese, oval eyes widened in subjective disbelief at what he saw and a few strands of his slick-gelled, tar-black hair fell across his sandy, yellow skin upon his brow.

And then he saw them.

"What the…?"

"GALEN!"

The sharp cry for help filled the air like the sound vibrations of a Chinese gong in an opera house. The unexpected arrival of the transporters in splattered shards of sprinkled garments left most of the onlookers shaken.

"Galen?"

He passed by the hooded girl in the crowd; her face barely visible as the lime-green, linen cloth shadowed over her features.

"Felix?" he whispered under his breath; the pumping factory in his ribcage picking up speed in the production line.

At the centre of the cobbled streets, in the five-metre wide, curved alleyway, knelt one of the men with stains of scarlet blood on his hands. Wherever they had been, one of them had clearly come back in a worse state. His hands became the lift-off platform from the ground, as he found his feet tracking from one end of the gathering circle to the other. His earth-brown eyes scanned the crowds like an image scanner in an airport security line.

The prints of sliding, red fingers still clutched on his dirtied T-shirt; pads of sand flew out of his sweat-gripped hair. The panting urgency of his breathing visibly grew, as if he knew every breath he took meant one less heartbeat for the one they had worked so hard for.

The well underneath his eyelids began to fill in desperation, and it showed, as both of his blotched hands reached up to his hair for a silent prayer of divine intervention.

Had all they had done and given up been for nothing?

"Ga…"

"Find Borus! Galen is probably in the apothecary and cannot hear us!"

The author of the doubly desperate instruction came from he who knelt over the wounded individual. Drizzles of liquid crimson scattered themselves across the midriff of his long-sleeved, mud-browned shirt that overhung slightly in the blaze of hysteria.

"We need to get it out Eli…"

"No! We could do more damage than it's worth."

"Don't just stand there! Find Galen!"

"He is losing blood with every passing…"

"Jero, you know that if we did that…"

A flash of light appeared consecutively with a silencing hush of the wind. A translucent, thin sheet appeared, standing firm in the midst of the crowded circle. As if born out of this watery veil, a pair of column legs marched out in haste. He landed skilfully out of the translucent portal door, and a barely noticeable ripple of dust billowed from beneath his oar-shaped shoes. This was probably due to the fact that this man stood at 230 pounds of muscle. Each lean piece of flesh created the bulky figure that confidently began to stretch upward from his slightly crouched position. His head was noticeably shaped like a bowling ball wrapped in pale white tissue; ripples of skin lining the back of his head. His bat-black jeans straightened out around his ankles in synchronisation with the straightening out of his whale-grey, tank top vest.

"All this commotion is abou…"

In that twinkling moment, as quickly as his teleportation entrance, he saw the reason for the treason of peace.

"Elian… Is that..?"

"Borus, not now! Find Galen!"

Borus flicked his arm up and down like a reloaded shotgun and, in the blink of an eye, a sharp, silver key appeared in the palm of his stubby, hairy hand. The head of the key resembled the tip of an avid arrow, and it narrowed its body until the oval-shaped hind was smoothly surrounded by the creases in his palm. He turned around in full understanding of what he needed to do and who he needed to find.

But did he understand the gravity?

A soft, female voice began to twinkle, in the dark atmosphere, from the brown-haired maiden at the front of the crowd.

"Fe…"

Felix's hand shot up, like a supersonic windscreen wiper, in her direction. His bark-brown eyes had not moved from where they currently lay.

"Stay back," he commanded in a short, sharp breath.

His chest was visibly rising and falling – sweat dripping from his brow – and as he did, Borus flicked his hand and fired the key at glistening speed in front of himself and towards Felix. Felix was now stood with his hands above his sand-tinted, navy blue trousers only a couple of metres away; his slightly pale face worriedly facing the crisis. Felix did not blink or twitch or look fazed, as the dart of death blindingly aimed to penetrate his skull. One foot away from his face, the arrow dissolved into the air; as if flying from one dimension to another.

Borus' stride inflated into a slight jog towards Felix, as the dissolved key translated into another watery veil. The transparent, vertical door hovered one foot above the ground; seven feet high; one metre wide. The thin sheet of paper became Borus' mode of intercession between any land and alternate realm.

He appeared to leap at full throttle speed towards the one in the blood-dirtied, white T-shirt. Felix began to place one foot slightly in front of him; proposing motion towards the other transporters and the wounded. In a fusion of time and space, Borus disappeared through the veil, which simmered into nothingness, and a multitude of grit and sand continued to fall down from the tyre-black, leather shoes on the cobbled floor.

"Fe… Felix? What is going on? What is the meaning of all this?" The young man in the mud-brown, fingerless gloves began. He moved forward towards the agitated man with caution and confusion. "Where have you been? Who is that?"

Felix walked like a transfixed zombie towards the nursing duo above the wounded. He was too wrapped up in the hurricane of his own thoughts to pay any attention to the outside world. All the commotion had obliterated the fact that they had successfully returned to…

"Felix!"

A firm hand gripped the hairy forearm of the man in the blood-splattered, white T-shirt. A cloak of sand, grit and watery sweat permeated in between the creases of the man's fingers. He pulled Felix's attention from the eye of the storm into the cobbled streets.

"Ja… Jayden…"

Felix looked at him with a mixture of disbelief and jubilation. To look into the windows of Felix's soul would answer all the questions you probably have right now, and Jayden wanted to know why on earth Felix was acting as if he was seeing a…

Felix abruptly embraced Jayden in a gallant burst of brotherhood. Jayden's streaks of hair fell upon his brow, as he juddered in the surprise embrace. His face was wrapped in confusion as he patted him on the back in response; looking around to make sure that the crowd was not wondering what this display of relief and greeting was all about, considering they had only been gone for a few minutes.

"Fe… is everything alright, buddy?"

"Felix." Jero's deep voice of caution fluttered like a swarming wind and rested in the ears of their recipient.

In a transformation of emotion, Felix cleared his throat, then choked up phlegm being swallowed, as he regained his composure and, looking at the ground briefly, as he stepped back slightly in the midday blazing sun, he placed his hand in a masculine manner on Jayden's broad shoulder.

"It's, er…" He sniffed and let out a brief undertone sigh, "it's just good to see you."

As Felix finished his sentence, a watery veil appeared behind him, and Borus stomped on to the ground, panting in urgency, closely followed by a bright-looking man. His hair was as a silver fox cuddled in patches of black moss trimmed neatly short. The trail of his sideburns stopped parallel to his oval ears and began again around his mouth. The rectangular millipede encircled his panting lips, as his deep, dark-blue eyes fasten themselves on, no doubt, what he was told he was needed for; his black, furry eyebrows contorting in concern. His ageing, cocoa-brown skin glowed in the golden rays, as his neck grew out of his night-blue, cotton, smart shirt. His seemingly planned dress code was somewhat awry with the Big Bird yellow, heavy-duty cotton shorts that his shirt was tucked into. Moving past the slim and lean legs, you were mesmerised by the red toggle sandals that wrapped his feet comfortably as he gently landed on the cobbled street.

"Eh, eh! What in the two realms?"

"Galen…"

"What have you done now?" Galen's West African accent filled the ears of the crowd; his arms flailing in the air. "I only sent you to get some bdellium from the sub-

Sahara as well as vincristine. I did not even have time to pick up my hat before being dra…"

"Galen, not now," Jero began. "Now is clearly not the time!"

Galen's wide eyes turned to face Elian and Jero. Their eyes guided him to the young man half smothered in a crinkled, sand-eaten and blood-dampened, mud-brown cloak that had once kept the wearer so warm in a previously written chapter of his life. His caterpillar eyebrows frowned in sad study, as he noticed the bruises and scratches that tattooed themselves in sporadic fashion over the boy's face. With eyes closed, the one noticeable flow was dried with clots of blood that wrinkled around his swollen, dark-brown and black nose.

The medic's blue sirens now focused on the broken shard that had ruptured itself into the boy's left ribs like a sword in a stone. The tip of the arrow, which had with lightning speed torn its teeth through his wet skin, was most likely clinging into the barely breathing victim's arteries closest to his heart.

"How is h…?"

"Shh, shh."

Galen clicked them to silence with his wavering hands. He then blinked slowly whilst taking a solid, deep breath; his hands stretched forward like a bishop laying hands on his flock. His once dark-blueberry eyes then flickered like electric-blue lightning.

"Borus…"

"I'm on it."

Borus once again reloaded his gun of keys in the background and, as he did so, Galen flicked his hand up in expectant motion. The arrow shot out of the motionless body and zoomed into his hand. The crowd gasped; each one trying not to be the distraction that forced the hand of mistake to claim another victory.

"Galen! What are you do…?"

"Eh, eh, eh!"

Galen lifted his index finger up in authoritative motion; waving it about in the air with each sound he made in his distinctive accent. The splintered arrow clinked on the cobbled street like a pencil dropped from a table in school. Droplets of red teardrops splashed from the marinated wood and into the tip. The same scarlet liquid was now seeping out from the deep wound where the splintered killer had dwelt. Elian and Jero had already begun to fumble about themselves for something clean to compress the wound.

"Galen! He's already lost enough blood, you old…"

"Eh, but you people!" Galen interrupted, scrunching his face in humorous disbelief. "You are acting as if I am not good at what I do!"

He began to crouch down to pick up the young man from whom he had just severed the relationship from the now still, broken arrow on the cobbled street.

"Good?" Elian's voice squeaked in pitch, as did his eyebrows. His eyes lowered to head level with Galen, as he crouched down and folded the damp, brown cloak around the boy. "Good!"

"Sir, what is the problem?" Galen's bright-white teeth showed behind his thick, black lips, as his nose scrunched like an old newspaper. "Don't you remember Valentina?" He rose up; boy lying motionless in his arms.

"Valentina?" Elian replied, rising up in unison with Galen.

"The one with the shoulder-length, black hair?" Jero asked, looking unsure at Elian with his finger pointing to the back of his head.

"Yes! Even that one!" Galen paced forward calmly towards the portal that Borus had so suddenly disappeared through.

From where Jayden was stood, one could just about make out that they were venturing into what would most likely be the place he was going to call home for the coming future.

"Galen," Elian retorted, "she is as mentally useful as a one-legged man in an arse-kicking contest!"

"Eh? But you are also mean!" Galen's head spiralled round; his face now baffled with exasperation at the publicly announced complaint. "The girl is fine!"

He nodded with self-assessment, eyebrows raised and bottom lip out in confidence, and began to place one foot through the razor-thin door into the indoor room on the outside.

"She… She has flipping bulging eyes! She looks like… like a tarsier!"

"Ah, ah, ah! Now! Do you know which plantation field flower cures anxiety from hippopotamus? Do you know the liquid to mix hypothenacithiumatomalium to serum 25621 in order to induce the right blood pressure for a man who has been pierced with a Laden's saliva-tipped, poisonous arrow? Can you take out the shards of these weapons and then continue to save lives?"

"Ga…"

"Ah, ah, no!"

"No Gal…"

"Eh!" Galen flicked his head up and down. "You do not listen!"

"Your er… your sh…"

"Ah, but you are now changing the subject! The answer is no!"

Galen kissed his teeth together, paused but then turned to Felix, Elian and Jero and smiled.

"But it is okay. I am Galen the Healer! And healing is exactly what I will do."

And with that phrase, Galen and the young man in his arms disappeared and the razor-thin sheet vanished into nothingness; the atmosphere in between the paper-thin door was joined once again. The last piece of cloth of Galen's corn-yellow shorts disappeared, along with the sight of a very visible, long tear of cloth from his left back pocket to his thigh which was caused, most likely, when he had knelt down to pick the young man up.

CHAPTER ELEVEN
Déjà Vu

A brief silence echoed in the air, as the dust tinkled on to the ground. The questions on everyone's minds were screaming; screaming, screaming out loud. But only the shuffling of feet made their voices heard.

"Felix?"

The soft tune from the young maiden's heart struck a fresh chord with the other, as the sound of his name snapped him out of the dazzling daze that he resided in. He felt her soft touch slowly warm over his damp hand which was clenched subconsciously, tightly around the scabbard of his sword. He blinked a couple of times in breathless speech, as his pupils regained a sparkle when he looked into the autumn-hazel eyes. His hand loosened, as his other rose to gently stroke her light olive skin.

"Fe..?"

She looked at him in loving confusion; eyes darting from one to another, as she then surveyed his torso covered in the mud and blood challenge he and the other two had ventured on.

"Where have you been?"

She had perfect posture; her head coming up to just under his nose. Her soft chin arched up to look at him, as her anxiety showed in the soft and subtle cherry cheeks.

"A... Ava."

The waterworks began to drip from his eyes, as he momentarily lost composure. As far as he was concerned, after all they had been through, this moment was one he had now got a second chance to share. He kissed her lovingly, and as he closed his eyes to do so, a conspicuous tear fell down his cheek.

"What day is it?"

Elian snapped into action, as he struck up his posture like a cautious pelican. He fumbled about his wrists in slight frustration.

"What…? What day..?"

"What day is it?" Ava brushed a flowing lock of her long hair and pulled away from Felix's embrace. "What do you mean what day is it?"

"Ava." Felix placed his hands on either side of Ava's arms. Her silky, baby-blue blouse hung loosely upon her shoulders, and her satin, white dress gently swayed ever so gently in the cool breeze that flowed through the crowded alleyway. "Ava, listen to me."

"Fe…"

"Ava… jus… please. Just listen. I'll explain some other time."

He looked around him at the crowd that was simultaneously eavesdropping on their conversation.

"But not here."

He looked into the windows of her soul in order to unlock a mode of unspoken communication. To tell her that there was a time and place for everything.

"But Fe…"

She lifted her arms up, to brush off the warm embrace of his hold, in defiance.

"Ava!" He gritted his teeth, trying to be patient and hold back the visions resulting in the waves of emotions that had brought them to this stage. "Ava, just trust me, damn it."

She looked at him with a mixture of discombobulation and disbelief. How could it be that the one she understood, the one she could so often read like a book, was turning out blank page after blank page?

"What has happened?" She carefully lifted her hand up to his trembling face and cupped it around his crackling cheek; dark fragments of hair from his ears rustled through her fingers.

"Friday!" Jayden called out. "Jero..?" He turned to him for some kind of answer. "Jero, what…?"

"What date? What year?" Felix's eyes darted themselves at Jayden in semi-frustration; his hands still firmly placed on Ava's arms, his eyes slightly bloodshot with tiredness.

"August. August 24th 2014!"Jayden huffed and puffed at the air after the rhetorical answer; arms returning to his sides from their trampoline departure. "What's wrong with you guys? Have you all been concussed or something?"

For the first time in this whole theatrical debacle, the three transporters were stumped for words, looking at each other as eyes crossed from one to another. Who was going to put forward the arm of reason first?

"We… we, er… We…"

"Eli!"

An intervening cry of relief cut through the crowd as did the maker of its origin. A beautiful lady bounced through the crowd. She stumbled across the cobbled ground into Elian's vision, and he let out a choked sigh of relief to see his hazel-eyed, blonde beloved run into his rising arms. Her plaited hair, wrapped in a network of hair clips, was the first part of her that Elian's nose rested in.

"Iris."

He embraced her, wrapping his arms around her sandy-brown, linen dress. He rested his cotton, damp, blonde, trimmed beard about her neck.

"Iris I…"

Elian began to be troubled by the same battle Felix had not so long ago faced.

"I love you. I've missed you. Are you okay?"

"I came as soon as I heard that you were back but something was wrong."

Iris moved her head slightly back to look into Elian's soft, green eyes. She didn't need to be an expert to know that her husband of twenty-one years was hiding something from her when she noticed the stains of blood and mud upon his clothes, and cuts and bruises on his knuckles. His bold, black staff lay on the cobbled ground, and she could sense the heat emanating from the golden ends. He had been fighting. Fighting somewhere, or something, powerful, and he had needed to use his abilities.

"Eli?" She paused and uttered to him as silently as possible, "Eli, what has happened?" She glanced at the stained blood on her finger. Whatever concern she had had doubled. Her light eyebrows danced in concentration and confusion, as the crimson stain was rubbed between her soft fingers. Perhaps, unlike her female companion, she understood that this was not the time or place to be visibly contentious. "You're hurt," she whispered.

"I'm fine."

Elian brushed his fingers across her rosy-red cheek. Perhaps putting on too brave a face in order to mask the slight tinge permeating from the gash in the lower left side of his back which caused him to wince every so often, he jerked himself in the hastiness of the situation.

"Don't li…"

"Everything is fine here, ladies and gentlemen!"

The commanding voice resonated through the internal thoughts of the still stampede which encircled the new guests in this realm. Jero's hands rose in the atmosphere to those around them; hoping to still the volume of questions, as his strong beams lowered and anchored themselves by his side. The blotch of blood stained the midriff of his bold, blue cloak which had managed to return its way to his back.

"We found the boy on our travels. The situation is not as grave as it looks. If anyone has any questions, we can discuss this tomorrow."

A murmur began to build in the crowd.

The chiming of the Guild bell vibrated in the ears of all those present, signalling simply that it was time to eat; and if you didn't get there quickly, you would be in that queue long enough to realise you should not have wasted time.

The crowd, like awoken victims of hypnotism, scrambled slowly but surely into the fortress, leaving a cold reception for those few who remained outside, the lack of questions answered leaving a slight chill in the air.

CHAPTER TWELVE
Rise and Shine - Part I

The glowing, uncomfortable heat radiated from my core. The gravitational pull of pain centred on the pulse of my beating drum that sent waves of blood around the tense and fragile tunnels of my body. The calm pressure upon my head was met with a cool, ever-present stimulus of liquid.

Water perhaps.

The gravity of subconsciousness tried to keep me planted in the void of sinking sand, and wherever or however I was, I was unable to fight it. I could faintly hear the discourse buzzing about my ears; that morbid illusion you debate the existence of when you are poisoned with fatigue and exhaustion.

"Hang on… so you… key?"

"…dead?"

"…gloves…"

I slipped in and out of a myriad of nothingness.

How much time had passed?

"…all of us? Dead?"

*** *** *** *** ***

"You know what's best?" Galen retorted, his hand stretching out into the middle of the quartet to break up what was turning out to be a rising crescendo in the patient's doorway.

"We need to have this conversation once we have all had a good rest."

Borus shook his head in disbelief, his pale eyebrows rising up; moving his forearms in puppet rhetoric at the insane suggestion coming from his comrade. You could tell Borus was agitated. The veins were showing in the temples of his bowling-ball head, and the widening of his pale-blue eyes, looking at the other companions to the conversation for approval, while being met with silence, was not calming him down.

"What is this rubbish! You tell me zhat you have lost your pow…"

"Borus."

Felix's soft, masculine voice cut into the conversation. He motioned his grazed hand towards Borus; not aggressively but in pleading.

"Borus, we can only tell you so much." His voice signalled a final plea before surrendering to fatigue. "I haven't even spoken with Ava properly."

He sighed deeply; a sigh indicating the effect the conversation was having on him.

He knew that he would have to have that truthful conversation with Ava, but would she understand? She was always one for principle. One for letting things be. Would she understand that he did this for her; for the plans he had for her, for them?

Borus, even for all his hardness of heart, could tell, just by looking at the emotional struggle Felix was poorly trying to hide, that what they had told him was not easy news. There were still many questions that remained unanswered, but he was more than aware of their need to rest. After all, they had sacrificed a lot for…

"You people! Are you in the business of sucking up the oxygen for the wounded?"

Galen was always one for hyperbole. His passion for his 'patients' was one that definitely showed.

Elian, on the other hand, was never quite sure whether Valentina would ever see his healing as a product of passion, but he did not doubt she was happy to be able to move again from her paralysed state! He smiled at Galen, as a short, sharp breath left his nostrils. A fold of his blonde fringe rested between his grass-green eyes.

It's good to be back, he thought.

"We were just checking on the lad," he said, waving his hand and head in the direction of the bed where the unconscious lay. As he spoke, Borus silently grumbled in the direction of the other two.

"Fine." He flicked his bulbous wrist with ease, and in Photoshop fashion, a chrome key appeared in the palm of his hand. His eyes met theirs. "I will help train the boy."

The key, no longer in the palm of his hand, fell from his clutch and descended like a teardrop to the floor. The tip of the nib-headed key dissolved through the stone-grey floor like a heron diving into the sea; shooting out of sight.

CHAPTER THIRTEEN
Rise and Shine – Part II

My eyes shot open, as I lay motionless in the soft material that rested over my body like a shield. As the haze fell from my eyes, the warm glow of golden streams to the left side of my face painted the ceiling as a dark amber motorway.

I could detect my heartbeat pumping within my chest, as my mind reasoned with itself.

Where am I?

In hospital?

What happened?

Is Mum or Dad…?

At that thought, the accelerator pedal pushed to full throttle in my veins, up to my mind, as a flash blasted in front of my eyes of a cruel claw of lightning that snarled in the billowing, black sky.

In a flash, I shot up from my bed; sweat beginning to seep from the pores of my brow. My chest rose and fell with every continuing riot that was physically, and mentally, taking place in my body.

The slightly damp, lilac, linen sheet crumpled down to my waist, as I sat up in the in large double bed. I glanced around me like a robin frantically looking for her lost young in a forest full of foxes. I noticed the dull yellow, stained-glass window a few metres in front of me that levitated above the oak wood door; a door that led into some sort of hallway. The room was fortified in silver-grey stone along the rustic walls, a pattern which seemed to be interrupted by the inviting fireplace at my left-hand side next to the long and tall window that the sun's face was peering into. Other than that, a grand-looking table and a one-metre wide, wall-sized mirror occupied the right-hand side of the mysterious room I found myself within.

I had to get out.

With my mind racing well ahead of my body, I peered under the linen.

Great, I was completely naked!

But I had to get out of here.

I glanced around the room (for some reason, including the ceiling) to see whether there were any clothes lying around. Minimum requirement: underwear.

Nothing.

I fumbled out of the bed; clasping the soft sheet as I did. But then a tight and uncomfortable internal slice pierced me from the left side of my ribcage and I winced, stumbling off the bed to be introduced, rather involuntarily, to the uncompromisingly immovable floor.

The emasculating splatter had only just resounded in the air when a high-pitched rebuke sizzled through the doorway.

"Eh, eh! What are you doing!"

Before curiosity had a chance to kill the cat, my attention was drawn to the now open oak door. A man stood there with eyes like blue lightning. His brown hands were raised to his silver head in amazement around a face which was glazed in disappointment and glee.

I squirmed like a worm on the cool floor; attempting to maintain as much dignity as possible while trying to reach out to the foam mattress to lift me up.

"Who… who are you?"

As if my words came out as a mime, the madman ignored my question and pranced towards me; his slippers flip-flopping on the soles of his feet as he motioned in my direction.

"But you want to give yourself a fresh concussion, child?"

I slipped, mid-rise, from the side of the bed and landed on my backside. Ready to face my chastisement, as the man's body blocked out the solar rays that were not absorbed by his eclipsed form, he surprisingly reached out to me an inviting hand.

"By the way, I have been rude."

A set of glistening white teeth glowed around the darkness of his lips and the silver bristle of his moustache.

"My name is Galen. I am the healer."

"The… the what?"

"The healer. Like a physician or a medicine man."

My mother had always warned me about 'medicine men'. She would often warn Jared and I, when we were in the Ugandan villages, to stay away from people whose houses were clad with chicken heads or who took a liking to staring like ghouls into the void of children's souls.

I unwillingly took his warm hand with caution; his bicep flexing as his long hand helped me to my feet, the linen sheet being clasped with my free hand by my torso.

"Er. Do you mean that you are a witch doctor?"

Galen's face retorted, and he slapped my hand away from his in a spate of disgust.

"A what? You think because I am a tall, black African who deals with potions and magic that I am a witch doctor!"

"I, er. I didn't mean to…"

Galen jeered and slapped his feet with his slippers in a two-step frenzy on the spot.

"Child, I am the one who saved your life. You think a witch doctor can do that?"

"Good morning, gentlemen."

From the other side of the room appeared what could only be described as a mercenary. If Galen was not going to kill me for calling him a witch doctor, this man certainly was.

His 'good morning' did not sound like one born out of politeness but more so out of frustrated necessity, as if my existence was causing him inconvenience!

His bulbous, bald head was the first thing that I noticed, as he heavy-footedly made his way to the drawers by the staircase of the room. He was fully cloaked in black and muddy-brown clothing from his neck to his dark leather boots. With eyes wide open, I noted the two daggers that lay about his sides.

"What are you doing here at this time, Borus?"

"I'm here for ze boy."

He impatiently scanned the drawers and eventually pulled out a white T-shirt, black trousers, a pair of night-black trainers and what I hoped was a pair of socks and some underwear!

"What do you mean 'for the boy'?"

"Jero, Felix and Elian asked me to…"

"Ah, ah! Anything they want you to do at this moment cannot be reasonable!"

Galen's face scrunched up like an old newspaper, as the bulky man by the drawers eyes', who had now started walking towards me, focused on mine.

"I don't make ze rules around here, Galen."

Galen stared with his mouth wide open in disbelief.

I, on the other hand, was still wondering how on earth he had got into the room without coming through the only entrance (and before you ask, I'd already checked out the window)!

In what seemed like an illusion, a moss-green-covered, sharp key glowed into appearance in the bald-headed man's hands. His chest rose slightly, as he began to pick up pace towards me.

"Hey, man, I don't want any trroouubbbllleee!"

He mercilessly threw the small incisor at me, and my eyelids clasped one to another. I glared my teeth in disbelief as my final bodily response towards this coward that would attack a fourteen-year-old boy clinging half naked to a bed sheet.

I felt no sting. No penetration into my neck or chest. What I did feel, however, was the surprising grasp on my arm that knocked me off balance and, in the process, knocked my grasp of the only shield of dignity I had left in this new world that I had awoken to.

However, as I involuntarily jolted backwards, expecting the next feeling to be my head cracking on the stone wall, I opened my eyes to see Galen rapidly zoom out of focus, his franticly waving arms like a highly irritated coach on the side-lines. I felt the unnerving somersault of my stomach, as everything around me blurred out of vision. The sort of vision you get when you stare blankly out of a fast-moving train.

Then, in a matter of seconds, it was all over.

CHAPTER FOURTEEN
Fighting Talk

Under the cool warmth of the beautiful light in sky, I found myself. Feathered about by evergreen leaves and the shade of the overhanging canopies, I ducked down like a meerkat cloaked in utter embarrassment at the lack of…

I was still relatively dazed at what had just happened. The roller coaster in my belly looped twice and, before I knew it, the convulsion ejected my head, to my side, right on to the man's shoe.

The awkward silence seemed to last a lot longer than it felt, but as I stared with rabbit-in-the-headlights eyes at his assaulted foot, the soft punch of clothes vibrated across my face.

"Get dressed."

"Wha… Hey! I'm sorry about… How did you…?"

"And when you're done, meet me in ze field."

Having dragged the clothes on hastily, I paced cautiously like Adam out of Eden into the outskirts of the thick woodland behind me. I could see a fortress of a building standing a few hundred metres away from me. The strong outside walls of this building stretched out to reveal many a window into the many rooms it held.

"What has just happened? What did you do? How did we get here? Am I…?"

"You are not dead," Borus interrupted, "if zhat is what you are thinking."

"But how…?'"

"My name is Borus. I am a key maker."

I stood silently staring at the man in enough confusion to hint that I had no idea what he was talking about. The cool breeze of the wind whistled across my face in stark contrast to the hard howl that shivered across my body at the beach.

The beach.

"What happened at the beach? My mum. Were those…?"

"…men who appeared at the beach real? Or were they just a figment of your imagination?"

A familiar voice beckoned behind me.

"Yes, they were very real, my dear lad."

"Y-You…"

"Allow me to reintroduce myself. I am Jero." He dusted off the clinging bark and twigs from his dark attire as he spoke. "Indeed, one should perhaps stick with the shortened version of my name, because the last time I tried to expand my full name you nearly choked on the very air."

I heard a childish snigger from Borus which was met with a hearty chuckle from the muscular-looking sage that stood before me.

"I… I remember you."

"Malaki…"

"It's Mala**chi**."

"Oh, I beg your pardon." He cleared his throat, as he stretched out the calf muscles behind his legs. "Malaki, there is going to be a lot you are not going to be able to understand, primarily because everything that you are about to experience is going to be… How do I put it?"

"Out of ze ordinary," Borus interjected; his silver dagger being juggled in his hands, as the sun's rays dashed off its face on to mine.

"Quite. One could say that."

"Deadly. Dangerous.

"Hmm… Well, yes…"

"Painful…"

"That's quite enough of your help, Borus."

Jero smiled kindly at me. In that moment of silence I felt like, so far, he was the only normal person around who I could potentially speak to who wouldn't shout or frighten me to death.

"I know you have questions; questions that need be answered. I dare say that there is a time and place for all things, my dear lad."

"Well, speaking of places, where am I?"

"You are safe. Borus here is going to train you, and you will work together for the next few of… well…" He stroked his woolly, white beard; perhaps trying to displace some nervous energy, "…years."

"Years! But I have to go find my…"

"Trust me, Malaki."

His tone changed from one of calm to one of a serious nature.

"If anything is certain about the future, my dear lad," he tapped his pale forehead and grinned, "I am sure to know it."

With that, he walked past me, patting my shoulder with his hand as he did so, and he headed towards the Guild.

So many questions spun a web in my mind. A part of me wanted to run into the enchanting-looking forest and be swallowed away from the place. On the other hand, I knew that I genuinely had no other place to go. I didn't even know where I was! One moment I was on a beach, surrounded by billowing winds and fog, the next I was in this peaceful countryside filled with weird and wondrous happiness. But one question lingered above them all. Who, or indeed what, was La Sombre Une?

"Head's up, kid!"

Snapping out of my daydream, I grabbed the foreign, linear object that was hurtling towards me with surprisingly good reflexes. As the brief flash from the sun dimmed from my eyes, I marvelled at the night-black scabbard that my hand gripped before fumbling to grasp the dark-blue pommel. With childish brain working in tune with curiosity, I chimed the scabbard off. I was not quite sure, in that moment, whether the shining light was from the sun or from the sword itself.

I clasped the black grip, as the sword stood proudly in my shaking hands.

"What is this for?"

"The creatures that we fight do not die from mortal weapons."

"The what?"

"We call them the Laden."

Borus' hard, blue eyes met mine.

"Creatures of death. Servants of La Sombre Une."

" 'Zeladen'? Really?"

"No. The Laden."

"Yeah. That's what I said. 'Zeladen'."

"No! *Ze*," The vertically chopped the air with his hand, "Laden."

And then I realised – Borus' accent was so strong the 'the' sounded like 'ze'!

"Ah! You mean '*The* Laden'." I paused my dystopian thoughts for a moment of brief self-congratulation. "Are you Russian?"

"Am I what?" His wide chest rose in an ignition of rage. "Russian!?"

"Oh. I didn't mean to…"

"Prepare to fight, boy!"

All 230 pounds of muscle began to pace towards me, the angry bull's steam fuming from his flaring, pale nose; his hooves digging into the ground, as he picked up speed towards me: his target.

"But I didn't…!"

Whoever said it was best to learn how to swim by jumping into the deep end either drowned straight afterwards or was the exception to the general rule of learning. Or such a maxim had a higher life expectancy than sword fighting.

Either way, Borus was coming at me. It was fight or flight.

And I couldn't fly.

CHAPTER FIFTEEN
Coming of Age

Descending balls of melting cotton fell from a frothy firmament. The fine flakes fell upon a glowing, white foam of a blanket upon the ground where my feet were firmly rooted in my dark leather boots.

The slight brush of moisture stole the attention of the nerves in my thumb, as the cotton faded into a clear tear which slid down my slightly frostbitten hand.

The cold air swirled through my lungs and transformed into a disappearing vapour, as I exhaled in slight fatigue. My arms were curved in front of me; hands holding on to sword while the silent hiss of the wind tiptoed in the open field. Promptly, the sound of crushed snow crept up behind me.

A crescendo of clatter ensued, as the portal from which Borus appeared closed behind him, his face mad with determination. His blade swept towards my head, but I ducked successfully. Suddenly the cold, hard hammer of his boot to my chest forced me to gambol into the thick, white blanket. By the time I was up (and wheezing slightly), Borus had disappeared again.

I fought back the neurotransmitter warnings around the bruised centre of my body; fighting back the reflexive well of water shooting towards the cliff of my eyes. Instantaneously, a frosty, sharp blade sat with precision against my throat.

"You lose."

"Well that depends, Borus."

"Depends on vhat exactly?"

"On whether you consider a sword point below *your* belt a loss?"

A brief silence echoed for a few seconds. No doubt Borus' ripped head had titled inconspicuously down to see his future generations at risk.

"I see…"

The silence abruptly ended, as he moved his dagger.

"I'll get you next time, Malachi."

He sniffed at the air, placing his trusty dagger into its scabbard at his left hip, looking around into the forest of Epoh and towards the Guild; perhaps trying to see whether there were any witnesses to our latest spar.

As far as compliments went, Borus was as giving as a pirate – but I would take that as a compliment for now!

Heading back to the Guild together, I reminisced upon the past three years that I had spent in the place.

Jero, as I had come to know him, was an exceptionally kind man. Throughout the years, he had helped me a lot to deal with the fact that I was away from my family. Frustratingly, he never answered all of my questions directly, and he always seemed to go off on a tangent, but I was sure his intentions were pure. There were plenty of times I would ask him and Elian where we were, and they would simply regurgitate a prolonged answer; telling me that there was a war coming that we had to prepare for and that they had saved me from a disastrous end at the beach.

Of course I was grateful. I still was now. I always would be. But sometimes, I thought they kept me too much in the dark.

*** *** *** *** ***

"Why do they call you the Future?"

Jero perched himself upon the edge of my bed; his posture perfectly poised. His clockwork tattoos spun around his forearm and into the shadow beneath his black, hooded top.

"Are you… from the future?"

His chuckle caused the soft foam mattress upon which I too was sat to vibrate.

"No, my dear boy, I am not from the future."

"Then why are you known as that?"

"I am known as Jero. That is my name. Well… in short. I am sometimes referred to as the Future because I can see it. That is my… well… gift."

"Your what?"

"My gift." He began to stroke his snow-cone beard in pensive thought. "I dare say mine is not always an exact science. I am presented with outcomes, or versions of what could possibly be ahead – but with all things concerning time, nothing is certain."

"But that's absurd. How can you…?"

"Know what is going to happen?" His paternal, blue eyes set upon mine and he smiled. "I don't know for certain all the time. I merely make a calculated set of decisions in order to try and either prevent the bad or maintain the good."

"Are there… are there more like you?"

"Like him?"

Another voice joined the conversion from across the room and towards the entrance. The speaker brushed a strand of his blonde fringe away from his brow, chuckling as he commented.

"No."

"Elian." Jero smiled and lifted up his hand in warm invitation to him.

Elian looked much different (at least in attire) from when I last saw him. In fact, they all did. None were prancing around in cloaks to begin with. Elian proceeded in a simple, cream-coloured, long-sleeved top and black denim trousers. What I wasn't too happy about was the fact that that he was walking into the room with muddy shoes!

"Oh," Elian must have read my facial expression, "I'll leave these by the door."

"And you are…"

A photographic flashback appeared before my yes. I remembered the encircling fog swirling around us, as the aura (or whatever it was) cleared my vision to see him standing in the midst of the gallant trio.

"…the Present?"

What was distinctly different about his man's appearance was the inch-long scar that had sliced dimly upon his left cheek.

"How did you…?"

"This?" He glazed his finger nonchalantly over his scar. "I ran into some friends of an old friend of ours. You can call me Elian, or Eli for short."

"I'm Malachi."

"Well, it's a pleasure to meet you under drier and less urgent circumstances, Malachi."

*** *** ||||||| ||||||| ***

Making friends here was always going to be a difficult start. I felt like an outsider in a foreign land; removed from my motherland without a choice and certainly without understanding. Everyone was just *different* to me. I did not know where I was, but I did know that it did not feel like home – and that was not just because everyone here seemed to have a 'gift'. Everyone would look at and study me, as I walked by, like I was some sort of alien object.

"Hey, Kai!"

Well, perhaps not everyone.

"How's it going, Harvey?"

Harvey was one of the first friends I made. He looked like your typical 'surfer dude', unnecessarily unkempt mop of sandy-brown, curly hair, good build and sporadically spontaneous. He even had one of those cheap strings about his neck with a clear-coloured amulet attached to it – and a peculiar one indeed.

"Cool, man. How about you?"

"Apart from the swelling of Borus' boot on my chest, I'm doing pretty well."

Harvey patted my shoulder, as we journeyed up the stone stairs towards the dorms.

"All is fair in love and war, my friend."

"Hah – yeah but with Borus," I rubbed my throbbing chest through the wet boot print on my cardigan, "there's no love involved."

"Well, wait till you take on Valentina. She's got some serious tricks but, dude, those eyes are serious!"

He gestured a measurement by clawing his hands and widening his hazel eyes; his furry eyebrows elevating under the canopy of his mop.

"Harvey," I said trying to control the contortion of laughter building up within me, "be nice! Speaking of which, you owe me a spar."

"Hah – the chosen one would like to battle Harvey the Hulk Warrior?"

He flexed his arms in a Superman pose; a cheeky grin permeating over his face.

"More praying mantis than hulk there, mate," I mumbled.

The friendly concoction of mindless banter filled the long, amber hallway.

He was one of the first people who spoke to me after my first spar with the bull (as I used to call Borus, as I could not remember his name). Having spent so much time training with Borus, I was yet to find out exactly what it was Harvey could do. Even after all these years.

CHAPTER SIXTEEN
The Sting in the Wind – Part I

"You should spend some more time with him."

Ava's sweet voice opened the next chapter of conversation. She gracefully walked around the simple pine dining table in her long, peach, flowing dress. The knocking of the white, circular plates upon the table in the brief silence hinted to him, as he sat a few metres away by the inviting fireplace, that his response was due.

"There's not much to say to him, Ava."

"I just don't understand what your problem with him is. He seems to get on well with most people here. Even Borus! And Borus barely gets along with anyone!"

From where Ava was inquisitively stood, she was unable to see the reflection of the dancing amber fire in his stoic, brown eyes.

"Or is there something about the past...? His past that you...?"

"Ava," he rubbed the frustration of the conversation out of his eyes, as he stood up from the wooden floor, "I have already told you there's nothing to say. If there was, don't you think I would have said it already!"

Ava paused for a moment in order to swallow the reflux of emotion that would have simmered the conversation into an argument.

"Fe, ever since you returned from, well, wherever in the realms it was you said you were three years ago, you

160

just seem to be so… tense and withdrawn most of the time. I just…"

"I know. I'm sorry. It's just… I…"

"Is it me? Is it us?"

Ava's voice choked slightly before she could finish her sentence properly.

"No, no, no. Don't be silly. Ava, I love you. I love you with all of my heart. It's just…"

"Just what, Fe?"

"This thing."

He brushed his hand through his slick, black hair, turning away from Ava and walking towards the fluttering embers.

"The past! It's… difficult to forget."

"I know that, Fe." Ava hadn't moved from the parchment of sunlight that was silently beaming through the open, French-style windows. The beautiful birth of spring had begun to peacefully foster the young buds.

"Ava, I need to tell you what happened before we came back with that lad. I need to tell you what had happened before, because it is the only way that…"

He paused slightly, pulling his head to one side and facing the floor; as if reliving a memory.

"Eli, Jero and I, we had to…"

Suddenly, a resounding blockade crashed through the young woman's home, and a cloud of dust forced its way into the living quarters and around the unsuspecting couple; sporadically mixing the brown and gritty cloud with shards of dangerous glass from the once immaculately clean dining room window.

"Are you okay?"

Spluttering and gagging filled a new void, as the spring breeze blew the sandstorm around the couple through the new opening. Ava's nodding head was hidden within the tight clasp of Felix's embrace; his hand waving the flying grit about his face to see the damage done to the side corner of the Guild where Ava's quarters were located.

"You…"

*** *** *** *** ***

Ten minutes ago…

The fresh tweeting of birds in the spring air was interrupted by Harvey's war cry charging in my direction across the open field. As he pummelled forward, his silver sword raised itself above his head in its latest bid to strike its target.

Me.

I felt the drumbeat within my chest pick up pace.

What options do I have?

Whatever options there were, I did not have time to consider them. A ricochet of blades connected and sliced in the spring air. I backflipped to avoid the almost likely fatal swoop of his weapon and, having landed, lifted my sword above my head to hear the instantaneous clang of his sharp blade against mine. With all the force in my body, I sprang up, uppercutting him as I did so, and as we both momentarily floated in mid-air, I turned full circle and forced a kick into his stomach that sent him gambolling on to the dew-covered, green grass.

He stumbled to his feet, breathing heavily, with sword in hand. I had landed on my sturdy feet; feeling a slicing pain across the side of my neck. Harvey flicked his soggy hair to the one side of his sandy-brown brow; spitting out a glob of blood and saliva from his mouth to the ground.

"You got me good there, Kai."

I wiped my fingers across the irritating tear in the skin of my neck.

Blood.

"You nearly took my head off!"

"Hah. Apologies. I got a bit too zealous there."

Tempus.

A soft whisper fluttered past my ear.

"What was that?" I whispered to myself; and looking down, I saw the ancient lines within my sword begin to glow a steel blue.

"Something tells me this fight is not over yet."

"Certainly not."

Harvey carefully wrapped his hand around the curious looking amulet that hung around his neck.

His eyes fastened upon me like a cheetah in the cover of tall savannah grass about to launch at its prey. The breeze about him began to quicken; encircling about him like a translucent tornado. His eyes then began to grey; his pupils being lost under the nimbus clouds.

"…Harvey…?"

"You wanted to know what my gift was, Malachi." He motioned his fine hand towards me; arm straight towards its target. "Now you will."

Tempus.

"What the…?"

"Separate!"

CHAPTER SEVENTEEN
Harvey's Past

"Together with this beautiful house comes this lovely garden, where I am sure you will enjoy many a BBQ in the summer sun."

The beautiful woman stood gracefully in her soft cream blazer and matching linen trousers, her inviting green eyes rested upon the recipients of her sales pitch, as she carefully removed a stray strand of her perfectly kept, brunette hair from her long eyelashes.

"It certainly is beautiful. What do you think, honey?"

The tall and slim gentleman glanced with controlled excitement towards his wife. She stood only a few metres away from him, standing outside the clear glass conservatory that elbowed out from the red-and-cream-bricked, semi-detached house. This place was exactly what they were looking for. With plans for another child on the way, there was not much to do with the place in terms of preparation.

"Yes, Stephen, I love the whole thing. I know Harvey and Bella will love it too."

"Ma'am, we will take it."

*** *** *** *** ***

Months had passed and the house was beginning to become a home, and nine-year-old Harvey and three-year-old Bella were part of the fan club. Harvey, in his sailor-striped T-shirt and corduroy trousers, crept quietly across the hallway by the front door. Surely his sister would not find him this time in their game of hide-and-seek.

He sheepishly tugged at his golden, curly locks as he wondered where to hide. Behind the curtains? No, too obvious. Behind the couch? That was the last place he hid. Bella may be young, but she wasn't dumb.

A natter of noise caught the young boy's attention.

Who was in the basement? One of Daddy's meetings that he had with those weirdly dressed people?

No. These were more like grunts mixed with female voices. Mummy?

Harvey quietly opened the wooden door to the basement which immediately compelled the traveller to wander down the flight of stairs into darkness. The murmurs were not clear; nor could he make out what was going on. He knew that if it was just the radio, or something, this would be a perfect place to hide. The only problem was he could not explain the dizzying shadows that danced like ghouls upon the basement floor.

The curious cat crept down the stairs; bending down cautiously at the nearest opportunity to peer through the gap where the stairs and the basement ceiling met.

The light was so dim that Harvey was unable to make out exactly what he saw. What he could discern was that there were at least two women there. In fact, one looked like the woman who was showing Mummy and Daddy around the house (but then again, many people look the same from behind), but the other woman's actions seemed more forceful and orderly; almost commanding. But who was she addressing?

Harvey could only make out a company of darkness from where he was crouching. With the lack of light, mixed with the slow rush of blood to Harvey's head, he could just about hear the one woman passionately patronise something, or someone, about a Guild and destruction – perhaps something about a realm too?

"I found you, Harbey!"

Bella's enthusiastic cry of victory filled the basement. Harvey nearly fell down the stairs at the surprising volume of her find. With heart beating fast and eyes open wide, he clutched on to the wooden staircase, as his eyes met those of the one woman who turned around to spot him too. He recognised her. What was that around her…?

"Harbey, I found you!"

Harvey turned like a scared cat up the stairs to see his beautiful sister holding the wooden door and pointing at him with a joyful smile on her chubby face.

He turned back to the basement floor.

There was no one there.

*** *** *** *** ***

The sharp scream that filled the house was undeniably from Bella. Harvey shot up in his bed; still frustrated at his parent's disbelief of his earlier account of who he saw in the basement but more bewildered at the cold, pale face of a hovering and rain-soaked lady in black outside his bedroom window. As the lightning struck across the thundering skies, her emerald eyes pierced through the condensation on the glass, and as sudden as the lightning's appearance, she was also gone.

Frightened and alone, Harvey rocketed out of his bed, and with the aid of his night light, managed to navigate his way to his door, intent on making a way to Mummy and Daddy's room.

*** *** *** *** ***

Swinging open my bedroom door, my little legs carried me past the door towards their room. On my hurried way, I hit something that was not supposed to be there. I thought it was Mummy, but instead there stood before me a weird-looking lady, outside Bella's room. She had the strangest of grey eyes. She looked like our neighbour who was blind. She was holding up her hand into Bella's room, and her other hand was clutching the thing around her neck that I think I had seen earlier. I could feel my heart beating really fast when I saw Bella floating in the air in the corner of the room by the ceiling. It was as if she was being carried away in a tornado.

I screamed for Daddy, but she instantaneously flung her hand in my direction. I felt so weightless, as I was forcefully thrown towards the stairs. Fortunately, the stair gate stopped me from tumbling down any further than I should have done, but I was in a lot of pain.

As I glanced up from where I lay, I saw Daddy come charging through and tackle the weird woman on to the floor, like the big men in rugby do. Bella came crashing down upon her bed; her blonde hair covering her terrified face.

The weird woman pulled out a big knife and put it into Daddy's stomach. Mummy also appeared and looked really shocked to see Daddy bleeding. I heard her tell Bella to hide under the bed and said something to the weird woman about not having me.

I have never seen Mummy so angry and attack someone the way she did; even though she had my little brother or sister in her tummy. But the weird woman was strong too, and she grabbed her necklace again and it looked like Mum flew into Bella's room. Mum didn't come back out though.

I fumbled downstairs, but the woman somehow appeared at the bottom of the stairs before I did. She looked up and behind me for a moment, and I did too, only to get a last glimpse of Daddy throw something and also be thrown (like I was) out of the window that was by the stairs. The clash of glass was so loud and terrifying.

Covering my ears, I turned around to see the weird woman who was looking pretty shocked. I could see the knife which she hurt Daddy with was now in her chest. She did not look pleased at all with her current situation.

The darkness in the house was now intermittently filled with blue, white and red flickers of light. I could hear sirens. The weird woman fell to her knees; letting go of the necklace as she did so.

I was so confused and so scared. These men suddenly appeared from the living room saying that we had to go. The oldest-looking one of them went to Bella's room. The blonde one waved his hand towards the front door and the banging, which was initially really hard and fast, was very, very slow.

I cannot remember much after that. I was just in shock.

*** *** *** *** ***

"I have slowed them down. We still do not have a lot of time."

"Where's…?"

"I'm here. We should go now."

"Yes, Borus, I was just about to suggest that."

*** *** *** *** ***

I do remember picking up the necklace the weird woman was holding.

*** *** *** *** ***

"What of Stephen and Victoria?"

"As I predicted, unfortunately, Felix, we were always going to be too late."

Jero, holding a scared Bella in his arms, came cautiously down the stairs towards the trio.

"Elian, would you mind sorting out the present circumstances before we go?"

"Of course."

*** *** *** *** ***

The last thing I remember were fireflies and feeling really like I was going to throw up, and leaving home very, very quickly. As if I had just blinked.

CHAPTER EIGHTEEN
The Sting in the Wind – Part II

A sharp and blurry, translucent-shaped sickle proceeded like a steam train through the air and in my direction. I momentarily saw how this aerial scythe cut the ground beneath us asunder like a fault line; a line which was fast creaking up in my direction.

I gambolled like a drunken antelope to the first side my shaking legs fell towards; the sickle narrowly chipping away at the clinging grass on the sole of my slightly mud-clung shoes.

Tempus.

"Harvey! What on earth was th…?"

Harvey twirled his hand about him toward me, causing me to feel the most stomach-wrenching feeling of weightlessness, as I flip-flopped upside down in a flurry of wind. Though the specks of dust were gaping ferociously at my eyes and the blood was helplessly rushing to my head, I was still able to see that my arrows had fallen out of their quiver which was currently knocking me across the face in this whirlwind.

As if I had taken a sharp turn on a roller coaster, I was flung to the ground; cascading upon the mushy ground.

Tempus.

Somehow, I had still managed to keep hold of my sword. Somehow I was hallucinating and contracting a form of hearing voices in my head. Why was it glowing? What was this 'tempus' nonsense I was hearing? I must have hit my head really hard!

"Head's up, Malachi."

Harvey's bantered warning refocused my attention causing me to realise that several sharp arrows, which had fallen from my quiver, were now facing in my direction a few metres in front of me; hovering ever so delicately in the air, held by invisible dart champions.

Harvey flicked a finger in my direction, and the first of the invisible champions thrust an arrow towards me.

Thankfully, all that training with Borus throwing daggers dangerously at me came to some sort of use. As if by natural reflex, I, with surprising precision, diced the arrow away with my sword; a wave of glowing blue trailing through the air, as I heard it whisper again.

Tempus.

I didn't have time to think. The next barrage of deadly arrows were coming thick and fast; being wielded by this wizard of the wind.

The flurry of arrows didn't seem to end. I felt a slice through my right arm where one of the arrows had slipped through my only line of defence; my wound beginning to bleed through onto my clothes.

All this training and fighting, was it really as necessary as they said it was? I know 'no pain, no gain' was a saying where I came from, but this was just nonsense! They kept saying that 'the day' is fast approaching, but what was that supposed to mean!

Connecting the blade of my sword with the tip of the windswept arrow, it flung at flickering speed into the nearby tree on the outskirts of the forest. Harvey still clung to the amulet around his neck; his eyes still raging with a ghastly grey.

"Let's call it a day, Harvey," I said, trying to catch my breath and enjoying a natural cause of wind in the spring sunlight.

He stood silently for a moment, perhaps contemplating his next move. I could feel the dull ache in my biceps, as I continued to clench my sword tightly in my right hand.

"That sounds like a good idea," Harvey said. "Let's head back to the Guild."

Satisfied (and somewhat relieved), I turned around briefly to face the rook of a building where I had spent the last three years. So much had happened. I had learnt so much. Why I was here? Why was all of this necessary?

Tempus.

And most importantly, the possibility that…

In what seemed like a flurry of seconds, I felt the rapid rush of wind racing towards me, felt the warm surge of metal and sweat clasp my tightening palm.

As I flicked my leg up instinctively in the air, executing an aerial cartwheel, wielding my sword with all the energy I could muster, for some reason the only word I could shout was: "Tempus!"

The sword began to cut through the shock wave that was only metres away from me. As if in slow motion, I saw the electric-blue veins within its bold body shine brightly. The blade of the sword morphed into a dazzlingly golden edge, and I could sense a power I hadn't realised before.

As I was engulfed by the shock wave of wind, I noticed that it all happened so, so slowly. I was rotating slowly too. Harvey stood there; the wind about him flustering through his floppy mop and grinning face. I turned to look above to see the birds in the air flapping ever so slowly; the armies of dirt and grass marching through the air beneath me at snail's pace.

What was this?

As the blurry tortoise of wind passed me, in the blink of an eye, it was as if someone had pressed the fast-forward button. So much so that the last of the shock wave flung me out of my cartwheel and to the floor.

The shock wave charged at supersonic speed behind me.

I belly-flopped on to the ground.

Facing Harvey.

His eyes back to normal; his face showing terror and regret, his arm still out towards its former target.

I had landed so hard, I didn't even hear the crunching clatter of brick, mortar and glass, or see the sandstorm of dust and grit that was cascading into the atmosphere.

The shock wave travelled behind me at speed alright.

Towards the Guild.

CHAPTER NINETEEN
The Sting in the Wind – Part III

Away from the mass hysteria that our actions had caused a few months ago, I limped cautiously towards my inviting bed and carefully lay down, letting out a silent sigh, perhaps because, after those events, even the inanimate objects in the room were still not offering to take my side and extend the solace of sympathy.

I glanced briefly at the scar on my right arm. The lacerated flesh had returned from a once swollen state to a thin, dark slice. Gazing quietly out of my bedroom window, and being mesmerised by the full moon and stars, I wondered whether Mum or Dad or Jared were having a safe opportunity to reflect on God's amazing creation in the same way I was.

Thinking about them again brought up the heaviest wave of loneliness, as I lay quietly in the lunar-lit room. I looked towards the dark, wooded table where the photo of my family sat. Jero had somehow managed, and kindly thought, to put the photo into a frame for me; to remind me that there was still hope.

He really was a kind-hearted and thoughtful man.

Perhaps the closest thing I had to 'family' here.

*** *** *** *** ***

I didn't have time to collect my thoughts. To consider a way to explain what had happened; or how it had happened. My heart was on a grand prix; my mouth wide open in horror, as I saw the smashed pocket of the Guild begin to be surrounded by people.

Although I clocked Felix charging towards me, I was in full realisation that Harvey had disappeared; nowhere to be seen. I scanned the forest like a pigeon scanning for the latest crumb at Trafalgar Square.

Where did he go? How did I…?

"Malachi!"

The latest shout of my name sounded sirens throughout my entire body. The hoarse shout from behind me merely served as a prelude to the forceful tackle of wind exiting my entire respiratory and digestive system.

Tumbling across the mushy field, even in my dazed state, I was sure that every part of my body had connected with the ground in some way.

"Get up!"

Felix's unforgiving voice broke the silence. He paced back and forth like an irritated lion in front of a disappointing pride; his coal fringe frantically falling about his brow.

"I said get up!"

"Felix. Wait, I don't know how it happened."

Clasping my aching ribs, I staggered to my feet as quickly as I could; trying not to show any sign of pain on my face.

"Pick up your sword."

"Felix… I…"

"Pick up your sword, Malachi."

His impatient tone began a nervous surge through my veins. The sort of feeling you get when the teacher calls you to the front of the class with the visible intention of chastisement.

"Or your last conscious thought will be praying that Galen gets here quickly enough."

With that, Felix charged at me – revealing his vengeful sword as he did so – not taking his eye off his target.

I'm not quite sure how to explain what happened next. The only thing I recall was a series of split seconds: noticing that my sword had tumbled unreachable metres from me; noticing that Felix had lifted his sword up in ferocious anger, and then lifting up my hands in order to shield myself (as if my arms were going to do anything useful in the first place).

I'm not quite sure either what surprised me first. The fact that all of me was intact; that one hand was firmly clasping the scabbard of my vagabond sword; that I had managed to block Felix's attack with my sword; the distant clink of metal echoing a silence in the now wide-eyed crowd encircling us; or that Felix looked just as surprised as I did.

"What on earth…?"

Time seemed to stand still. Our voices had intertwined with the same question to the other about what had just happened. With my wide eyes fixed on the crossed junction of metallic blades, my eyes moved to Felix's face; the adrenaline factory within me beginning to overflow.

My sword had returned to its normal silver state. No whispers. No glowing lights. No synergy.

*** *** *** *** ***

The bass in my chest beat faster at the remembrance of that moment on that day – November 17th What I couldn't figure out was how it had happened.

Why it had happened.

In any event, Felix was so blinded by impulsive anger at me for endangering his girlfriend that he did not even give me time or room to explain.

I suddenly realised a dull ache had begun to seep from my jaw. Releasing the crocodile clench on my teeth, I turned in my bed to face the window in the darkness with an invisible frown upon my brow.

*** *** *** *** ***

Felix, like a possessed python, came in thick and fast with his spitting strikes. The crowds began to gather around us like a swarm of bees to the last sweet scent that the golden drop of honey exudes, the faint gasp and buzz echoing at every dodge; every swift separation of the air.

"You are just a spoilt brat, Malachi…"

Felix was too strong for me though; too experienced, too angry. The lactic acid had built up in my limbs; my arms and legs beginning to fatigue at the constant need for defence.

"…who doesn't know how to control himself and act like an adult!"

At one final, strong swing of his weapon, my sword blasted out of my hands. The tingling vibration sizzled my fingers and sent a wave of faithlessness into my ego. Felix's unforgiving eyes locked on to mine like a lion about to deliver the final blow to the lame fawn.

Every feeling that I had been suppressing in that moment came to the surface. Nothing mattered any more. No one mattered any more. Felix had publicly made me feel like I was the single-handed cause of everything that was wrong in the world.

"What has gotten into you?"

I clenched my fists and didn't blink, as I returned a channelled gaze of frustration into his burning eyes.

"Every step that I take is another mistake to you, Felix!"

My temples violently massaged my skin, as I ignored the pain that built within my jawline.

"You took part of the Guild out, you irresponsible git! You could have hurt…"

177

"You don't know what happened! You just charged in like a drunken bull at me without rhyme or reason!"

Felix's face loosened, as the spirit of anger began to dispossess him.

"Well," I began, bowing down sarcastically, "I'm sorry, oh Felix the great."

"Oh, you think you're a comedian now you…"

"What is the meaning of this Felix!"

A familiar voice spoke behind me. Felix would have seen who the outspoken spectator was, but my eyes stayed on Felix.

"Yes, Felix. Yes, I think it's flipping hilarious that I have had no control over anything that has happened in my life; to my family, my friends, my home."

The buzz of the bees subsided.

"Did it ever occur to you that I'm tired of being what you want me to be? I didn't ask for this Quantum bull…"

"Malaki! Enough!"

*** *** *** *** ***

It was probably for the best that Jero came when he did. Swords and stones may cut my bones, but my words were about to detonate. Lying in my warm and comfortable bed, the sweet hymn of silence…

CHAPTER TWENTY
Sweet Dreams - Part I

Loud, multiple snaps of twigs underneath my naked feet clicked into my ears, as I casually walked.

The beautiful, fresh flow of air filled my empty lungs, taking in a wave of freshly blossoming lavender. The soft flow of life in the nearby distance played so beautifully in my ears. In this mesmerising playground of brown, green and a mirage of colour, the calming aerial streams of golden rays fell from the heavens; playing dot-to-dot on the forest floor.

I had never felt so free.

I playfully chased an elegant, multicoloured butterfly, skipping across a fallen lump of log as I did, until it flew up into the colony of canopies; joined, perhaps, to his significant other, as they spiralled in union out of sight, out of reach.

In this Garden of Eden, everything was so peaceful; so calm.

I found a conveniently outstretched and low branch fitted on a bulky tree, its skin teaming with wrinkles and veins with all manner of workers scurrying about its bulky stem; each male seeking a prize for the queen. Embracing the still invitation, I eventually found myself basking in a pocket of heavenly warmth.

With eyes calmly set upon the nearby white and clear flow of life; droplets pitter-pattered upon the marble and grey protruding fingers in the earth. Green moustaches playfully showed upon the faces of some of the rocks glistened intermittently, as a droplet reflected a hint of the rainbow that mystically relaxed in this tranquil paradise.

"Oh, to live forever would be beautiful…"

The wind carried a beautiful voice which strung hypnotising chords in my ears, trailblazing like a forest fire into my warm heart. Like the scent of a warm, home-made dinner to a tired man aroused from his sleep, the tune swung an intoxicating noose around my neck and summoned me; as if I was jinxed by a Pied Piper.

The soft tweeting of birds harmonised with the mesmerising tone to which I was coming closer.

So clear.

The beautiful hum led me through the paper trail of the Creator's handiwork. A swift sparrow seamlessly glided through the rainbow obstacle course of nature, closely followed by a flock of blue and grey-crested kingfishers; hints of beautiful, white dots sprinkled upon their wings with each hurried flap into the forest.

"Oh, to live…"

So new.

Along the brown, dirt track that I walked upon, I heard the familiar splash of flowing water nearby. Looking up to the sky momentarily and closing my eyes, the golden rays of sunlight lit a soft red and orange glow under my eyelids; I wanted to just remember this moment forever.

"…would be beautiful…"

Soft light splashed into my eyes, as I opened them to find myself by a natural pool of clear water. Graceful arrays of yellow and orange danced upon the reflection of the water. The water fell from a few metres above – the mouth wide open upon a stony edge – gushing into the calm and cool stream.

"Oh, to live forever would be beautiful…"

Sat gracefully upon a smooth, large stone, the woman carefully caressed her beautiful, long, black hair. It flowed down, swaying gently in the wind, to one side of her neck. With one left foot dipping reminiscently in the steady stream, she combed her fingers through her hair like she was playing a harp to her beautiful tune.

She wore an unforgettably white dress which contrasted so well with her glowing, ebony skin.

Her eyes met mine, as she finished another tune.

There was a moment where I felt a bit rude for staring, a bit weird for just bashfully standing there. Regardless, this woman sung beautifully and strangely, there was something about her that reminded me of my mother.

She effortlessly alighted off the rock she was resting on and began to walk towards me. Although probably in her forties, the woman looked radiantly fresh-faced and youthful in her gentle smile. She played a few strings of her hair, as she came closer to me; smiling as she studied behind the window of my soul.

"I… I'm sorry to interrupt you."

When she reached me, she didn't stop moving. Instead she began to slowly pace around me.

"I just wanted to let you know you have a very beautiful voice."

The fresh smell of wild flowers lathered into my senses as she did so.

She stood in front of me; probably around 5 foot 9 and slender in body. I had only just noticed the golden-brown, laced girdle about her hips which interestingly matched her captivating eyes – the strings gracefully tinkling quietly in the soft breeze – that were studiously looking into my own eyes.

"Thank you, Malachi."

My eyebrows wrinkled, as a cautious gulp treaded down my throat.

"How do you know my name?"

She didn't flinch or falter, remaining calm and poised upon the stream's bank.

"I know many things, Malachi," she began, as she started to slowly pace about me again. "Me knowing your name should not be your concern."

Something wasn't right. Having taken my concentration away from the woman, I noticed that dusk had all but too quickly settled in, the creepy clicking of the crickets had begun phase one of their opening act. Pockets of fireflies began to gather in mid-air blotches throughout the distant woody abyss.

She chuckled a single breath into the silent atmosphere.

"My... how you have grown, Malachi," she enchantingly commented, as she passed by my left side, walking a few metres ahead towards the stream; staring, perhaps, into the flowing water.

"Who are you?"

I interrupted the growing silence, placing my hands to my side to clasp my sword should the need arise.

My sword...

I felt my heart slam a bass note through my chest; the undeniable lack of space between my palm and my denim shorts confirmed.

In the growing angst, I noticed that the several sparks of light coming closer to us were undeniably not fireflies.

"What is the matter, Malachi?"

She stood in the same position, still facing away from me and towards the stream.

I had heard of these creatures before. Borus had warned me countless times of the need to train and prepare for...

Instantaneously, slithering twigs blasted from the ground, like beanstalks encircling about my legs, and began attempting to pull and drag me towards her. I had managed to instinctively kick one foot up in the air in time, however, the earth had wrapped her veins around my right leg; digging their nails into my flesh.

These carried the face-wrenching smell of death.

"Are you scared?"

I slammed on to the ground in the dim dusk. Sparks of dust flew into my eyes and nostrils. Fallen shreds of bark flew into my open mouth and latched themselves on to the back of my throat, leading me to cough and spew; the harsh scratching causing a burning sensation in the back of my mouth.

I frantically and desperately tugged and clawed at the earth's veins about my now bleeding leg; clumps of dirt and soil clung to my throbbing fingernails.

They were here.

She stood in the same position.

But how?

Still facing away from me and towards the stream.

They were here.

"You should be."

The Laden were here.

CHAPTER TWENTY-ONE
Sweet Dreams - Part II

Clouds unforgivingly covered the pale flint of the foggy, white torch above.

A branch broke nearby.

A gargle of distain was close to my ear.

An echoing roar filled my senses and immobilised my stinging legs for a split second.

I fumbled and fell into the earth.

The sick cry of a deranged baby shot through the atmosphere.

I ran.

"Oh, to live forever…"

I had to run.

The skeletal fingers and limbs of the canopies above ached disturbingly and contorted towards the earth.

A cottage.

About a hundred metres from me.

A flurry of heavy footsteps caused the earth to tremble.

"…would be beautiful."

The crowds of crickets still stole the air in an orchestra of eerie composition.

My lungs were burning like a volcano. My eyes were…

The creepy crushing of dead leaves was heard nearby.

I stopped in my tracks behind the spiralled spine of a naked tree. I tried not to breathe too harshly, tried to quieten the thumping crescendo in my chest. The mist appearing from my breath in this demonic nightmare would only serve to betray me.

Hunted, I peered cautiously around the decaying spine.

The coal-black beast paced about the forest floor. Its skin seeped oils producing slick fur that armoured its tank-like physique. Its blood-stained head turned towards me; whispers of fog twirling about its bovine head as it did.

"Oh, to live forever…"

I could hear its heavy breathing getting closer.

Three.

A thundering step vibrated in my direction; causing small bones from the tree I was pressed by to fall and fumble about my shaking body.

Two.

The unholy grunt and dark purr of the beast simmered closer.

One.

I could hear the drops of red liquid drip from its bone-white horns on to the desperately dry leaves.

A petrifying roar crashed into my ears.

I darted like a hare out of its burrow.

The stampede quaked behind me.

Leaping over dregs of logs like a cheetah across the plains.

"…Would be beautiful…"

Splashes of moonlight illuminated my way through the obstructive fog and mist.

The whistle of a crude oil arrow darted past my head and punched into the darkness in front of me.

Scrawny fingers of the forest dwellers unsuccessfully grappled at my throat; this dystopian snow-white forest acting as a mercenary of madness.

The swarms of fireflies were multiplying behind me and all around me.

"…to live forever…"

Into the vulnerable open compound I descended, ignoring the wall that my muscles had hypothetically hit.

The cottage looked empty.

I restrained from obeying the loud cry of my overheating head telling my body to stop.

The lights were on.

I noticed a golden girdle.

The huge, thick door was closed. No doubt locked.

An illuminating white dress on the other side of the forest.

Another coal-black arrow pinched the ground where my naked foot had only milliseconds ago departed.

A window.

"…would be beautiful…"

As if competing for gold in a gymnastics final, I leapt, fists first, through the shattering window. Shards of glass impaled my fists, face and legs, as I gambolled into the dusty, empty, open-plan cottage. Like an injured gazelle caught by her impending prey, I realised that this building was the only armour between me and them outside.

Now, there was only deafening silence.

The falling icicles of glass from my flesh, as I picked myself up, were the only sounds that could be heard.

No tune.

No song.

Just silence.

I didn't even know what had happened at the stream.

All I remembered was that one moment I was being dragged towards the woman by the stream by twigs blasting from the ground and, having clasped shut my eyes in desperation and fear, I'd opened my eyes to find myself in the silent shade of the night in the decaying forest.

A barrage of battering rams shook the steadfast door.

"YOU CANNOT ESCAPE ME, MALACHI!"

This was it.

Dust shot from the cracks in the door, as the barrage continued.

"YOU CANNOT CHANGE YOUR DESTINY!"

A creak. A shudder.

"I WILL FIND YOU!"

A crack.

My pulse quickened.

"I HAVE DONE IT BEFORE."

Sweat flooded from my pulsating brow.

"THEY CANNOT PROTECT YOU FOREVER!"

A piece of the door shot across the stone-cold cottage floor.

"What do you want from me!"

A devilishly red glow echoed through the growing gap of the door.

"What do I want?"

The whole wall, as well as the door, crumbled like the walls of Jericho in the days of Joshua. The cold sting of the night pinched at my bruised and cut skin, as the misty clouds of fog lazed over our feet.

"You foolish boy. Your incompetence belittles you."

She appeared.

Although dressed in angelic white, her soul was black as the night.

She, without taking her vengeful eyes from me, flicked her hand wickedly to her side.

"That question I can answer."

Her golden girdle slithered from her like a serpent; levitating insidiously in mid-air. She shot her hand at me with full force. The golden serpent darted towards me instantaneously.

"I WANT YOU DEAD!"

Malachi will return...